Dead Letter:
Addressee Unknown

Janet Feduska Cole

PEGASUS BOOKS

Pegasus Books
3338 San Marino Avenue
San Jose, CA
www.pegasusbooks.net

Published in North America by Pegasus Books. For information, please contact Pegasus Books c/o Caprice De Luca, San Jose, California, 95127.

Dead Letter: Addressee Unknown/Janet Feduska Cole – 1st edition
p. cm. First Edition: May 2014
Library of Congress Control Number: 2014907003
ISBN – 978-0-9910993-9-9

1. ANTIQUES & COLLECTIBLES / Stamps. 2. FICTION / Action & Adventure. 3. FICTION / Thrillers / Suspense. 4. HISTORY / Holocaust.

10 9 8 7 6 5 4 3 2 1

Comments about *Dead Letter: Addressee Unknown* and requests for additional copies, book club rates and author speaking appearances may be addressed to Caprice De Luca or Pegasus Books c/o Caprice De Luca, 3338 San Marino Avenue, San Jose, California, 95127, or you can send your comments and requests via e-mail to jancolemail@comcast.net

Printed in the United States of America. Also available as an eBook from Internet retailers and from Pegasus Books

Acknowledgement

Thank you to Pegasus Books,
And all my family and friends,
in particular my husband, Ed, and
My sons, Drs. Russell and Andrew,
For their enthusiastic
encouragement and support.

"Life is either a daring adventure or nothing."

Helen Keller

DEAD LETTER:

DEAD LETTER: CANCEL POST UNIT
UNITED STATES POST OFFICE
SAINT PAUL, MINNESOTA 55101-9651
OPENED, PILFERED

POSTAGE DUE   29   cents

Addressee Unknown

Dead Letter: Address Unknown

following

Cancelled: *Stamps to Die For*

By Janet Feduska Cole

Elyse, Saul, and Arturo continue their unrelenting quest for the Lünersee stamps. Clues arriving in cryptic envelopes have expanded their search interests to include other priceless artifacts stolen during WWII. The Amber Room, an invaluable treasure stolen from Russia by the Nazis, tops Elyse's list.

After completing a philatelic cruise, the trio evades a deadly crash scenario, initiated by a sinister driver on a European highway. Another attempt upon their lives occurs on the shores of Lake Lünersee. The adventures continue into an underground cavern where their survival is uncertain.

Dead Letter:
Addressee Unknown

By Janet Feduska Cole

Chapter 1

I savored my temporary respite. Pushing the treasure-hunting travails of the previous month aside, I engaged in more frivolous, family-oriented activities. We shopped. We hiked. We enjoyed the spectacular southwestern scenery, and we dined, and then re-dined, and shopped again. *Alleluia!*

Soon after returning home, vacation bliss receded. The stamp quest again became my primary focus. For the unfamiliar, I had engaged in an unsuccessful attempt to find a collection of precious stamps stolen by the Nazis during WWII. This treasure was thought to be buried near Lake Lünersee, Austria. It was a quest that I hoped to resume.

Some plans never materialize. Some plans are aborted. Mine came to a screeching halt when jury duty reared its disruptive head. I responded with reluctance to the summons. This was not my priority. To all who would listen, and there weren't many, I threatened to appear at the preliminary screening wearing a bunny costume.

I would scurry across the floor in my ridiculous outfit while carrying a briefcase, crying out,

"I'm late, I'm late..."

I was *hopping* for an early dismissal. Get it? Alas, few—well, no one saw the humor in my pun.

When the day of reckoning arrived, I became not a rabbit, but, instead, a chicken. Abandoning my initial plans, I dressed in almost respectable corporate IT attire (jeans and a sweater).

****

Jury duty in the Chicago area is a unique experience. Before coming to the courthouse, we, the summoned, read our instructions and then checked the official website twice a day. With this method we could determine if a morning or afternoon appearance were in order. The first two attempts to access the site were unsuccessful. An electrical failure was the culprit according to the recording at the number we called when we couldn't access the website.

After a day's delay, I arrived at the courthouse. I no longer felt unique for having been selected. There were more than 80 people marking time in the huge room serving to warehouse the prospective jurors. We were of all ages and from all walks of life, a fact that became even more evident later in the process.

Some were wise enough to bring books, Nooks, or Kindles to pass the time. Others stared with glazed eyes at the variety of inane programs offered on the wall-mounted flat-screens. I sat back feeling somewhat superior because I had brought with me both a Kindle and a sandwich.

Bye and bye, a clerk appeared just long enough to advise everyone to indulge in a two hour lunch break.

"Break from what?" a bored sounding voice muttered from behind.

For those unfamiliar with the surrounding area, there were no obvious hang-out spots. Rather than wander unfamiliar deserted streets alone, I returned to endure, alone, my un-garnished cheese sandwich from home.

Just as I reentered the now vacant jury room, a figure, face obscured by a hoodie, jostled me while rushing past. Sensing that this was no accident, I turned to glare. The figure had vanished, but the echo of footsteps lingered in the deserted hallway.

Other jurors soon trickled back. Presently, a bailiff appeared and began calling identifying numbers. Many seemed as clueless as I, not knowing how to interpret the numbers on our badges. After scanning and screening us as though we were items on a supermarket conveyor belt, the bailiff packed us into available elevators. He then gave instructions to press floor two, the site of the court rooms.

By some odd circumstance, I landed in an elevator occupied by an individual attired in a long black coat and a fedora. We were alone. Where he had come from and why no one else was in the elevator gave me pause. There was no way that he (or she) had been in the waiting room with the other jurors. I would have noticed. A scarf obscured most of the stranger's face. I sought eye contact to determine if conversation were an option. The returned glance was cold, sinister, and familiar.

The elevator lurched to a stop on the second floor. Unnerved, I stumbled as I sought security among the other jurors. When the elevator's door closed and began its descent, the stranger in the long coat and hat remained its sole occupant.

After lining up and counting off two or three times, the prospective jurors entered a courtroom where an amiable judge instructed us on proceedings and decorum. She interviewed the potential jurors in groups of four, identifying us by our numbers and then asking each prospect the same boring and repetitive questions.

The queries were for the benefit of the two participating parties—the prosecution and the defense teams. Based on our answers, one or the other would either accept or decline the prospective juror.

The prosecution consisted of a tall, waspish-looking attorney and his tall, similarly-waspish-looking female assistant attorney. Both sported expensive courtroom attire.

The defense consisted of two women, an African American and a Latino, as was the male defendant. Their attire and demeanor were conservative. The contrast between the opposing sides was a stark one.

The jury members were diverse. In my heightened state of awareness, the great contrasts among the jurors seemed hilarious. A female cop on my right sat beside an admitted convicted felon. He had served time either for burglary or domestic violence. He couldn't remember which. To my left sat a gun enthusiast. His proclamation to the entire assemblage was loud and passionate,

"I'm a member of the NRA and I *love* to target practice."

The prosecution dismissed him.

Next to the gun guy sat a paramedic who seemed to satisfy the criteria of both the prosecutor and the defense.

Perhaps each team hoped to appeal to his compassionate nature.

When the time for my interview approached, I felt agitated. I was tired, nervous, hungry, and resentful. Why was the accused, a rough-hewn hombre, glaring at me? Rather than becoming intimidated, I reciprocated by glowering back.

The defendant allegedly threatened the accuser with a gun while on his property. All the while, the defendant scowled, as did I. Did I know him? There was a feeling of *déjà vu*. After answering a tirade of questions, much to my shock, the defense attorneys rejected me as a juror.

"Why?" I asked myself. "Was my hatred of guns that obvious? Perhaps I should have refrained from making disapproving faces at the defendant. Ah, well! Hindsight!"

I would have enjoyed the interaction with the other jurors and listening to the attorneys practicing their craft. Disappointed, I slunk from the court room.

What a relief to be the only occupant in the elevator. There was no one to witness my embarrassed sulking, the result of being pronounced unsuitable for these particular proceedings. The elevator accelerated with amazing swiftness for descending only one floor. Return trips always seems quicker.

The lift landed with a neck-wrenching jerk.

Well, th-th-that's all, folks, I thought as I left the courthouse, looking around at the abandoned streets.

Chapter 2

The up close and personal exposure to the law, however brief, reignited my enthusiasm for solving the Lünersee stamp mystery. There was enough injustice in the world. We shall find the stamps return them to the rightful owner's heirs.

The jury duty experience did renew my feelings of discomfort, or paranoia, if you will. I had difficulty determining if the day's strange encounters, when coming through the courtroom door and in the elevator, were coincidental. Or was someone once again tracking me.

Nevertheless, the stamp quest would continue. And I would either avenge Karl, or wreak revenge upon Karl, whichever strikes my fancy at the time. Justice must be served!

The Lünersee stamp mystery remained just that—a mystery. I retained a copy of the map inserted into my purse by an unknown party during my trip to Sweden.

It was a reminder that while many persons were obsessed with the same quest, none had displayed a desire for direct camaraderie or collaboration. Rather, ruthless interlopers lurked in the shadows, determined to find the elusive stamps before others. Having, in some cases, dedicated half a life time to this pursuit, they were uneager for competition.

The one exception was the person(s) who had inexplicably left the clue for me. Other clues included Karl's cryptic note, which indicated that Karl and his father had possessed, but then reburied, the stamps in their original hiding place.

Why should I succeed when so many before me had failed? Were there those deluded enough to think that, with the proper information, I could solve the mystery? Were they depending on me to lead them to the elusive Nazi treasure alleged to be hidden near Lake Lünersee in Austria?

Whatever! I was ready for the merry chase to commence.
I felt confident that I would once again evade my enemies.
My explorations would succeed.

Chapter 3

Life is a series of overlaps. Personal adventures often enhance a career and vice versa. My assignment of researching and writing an article about philatelists for Arturo's magazine provided both the stimulus and the perfect cover for conducting the Lünersee stamp quest.

Disregarding the delay created by my brief stint as a prospective juror, the quest had run into certain roadblocks. There was the unproductive, but still interesting, interview with esteemed European philatelists, Jürgen and Walder, two unique relics from the World War II era. These were individuals who no doubt have, but refuse to share, intimate knowledge of the Lünersee stamps' existence and fate.

I was dissatisfied with the vague reassurances provided by my previous companions. Arturo, my Polish-born editor, had recently made the conversion from print to becoming an on-line publication. His focus was on making the magazine's evolution a success.

Saul, an eccentric archeologist and petroglyph expert employed by the Chicago Field Museum, was preparing for a large exhibit. They both claimed that the three of us would recommence our search *very soon*.

Since they provided no substantive information or an actual date, I began to evaluate options. I could wait with unaccustomed patience to hear from those two nebulous characters, or I could adhere to my instincts to trust no one and to strike out on my own once again.

My faithful contacts here in Chicago, Pittsburgh and Washington DC were still primed and ready to lend remote assistance. There was no reason for me to linger, forfeiting to others the time to act upon the clues we had risked our lives to discover.

I checked with the museum. Saul was working hard on his complex petroglyph project, a magnificent recreation of the 20,000-year-old drawings that had been discovered in the Lascaux Caves in France. This exhibit would on display in the Chicago Field Museum very soon.

As for Arturo, it appeared to be business as usual with the magazine. Within the last week, he had delivered more assignments than was typical. Those, in conjunction with my article on philately, amounted to a hefty work load.

The wheels of cynicism resumed turning. Were these assignments simple ploys to keep me busy and distracted? Arturo could be communicating from anywhere, even Austria.

Then again, I could do the same.

Chapter 4

Outside, beyond the deck, a little robin relaxed in the birdbath. After several moments, she rallied and began splashing her wings to rinse away the residue from a day of hungry worm foraging.

The distraction was but momentary as I once again returned to my musings. Sprawled in a deep leather chair, one toy poodle hanging over the armrest, the other snuggled in my lap, I pondered a most recent development.

My sources indicated that Karl, my former college acquaintance and his accomplice, Mindy Slutkowski, often referred to by me as slut-woman, had married. Birds of a feather and all that, they were taking a brief respite from tracking me tracking the stamps to enjoy a European honeymoon aboard a luxurious Danube River cruise ship complete with philately activities.

In keeping with the modern tendency to conjoin the names of famous, in this case "infamous," couples, I shall now refer to them as the *Slarls,* a combination of slut-woman and Karl.

My sources also revealed that the Slarls' cruise would be pausing for a layover in Austria. A shiver of apprehension traversed through me.

It was my suspicion that the allure for traveling to those regions was not the Edelweiss, nor the Bavarian beer. The Slarls were pretty keen on beer, but their fascination, I was quite certain, lay within the Lünersee Lake region. It was a legitimate concern that the ship's agenda would provide them adequate time to explore the area where the stamps were thought to be reburied.

But why on earth did they wish to discover the stamps before I did? It made no sense. It had been my theory that I had been duped into participating in this hunt so that I could locate the stamps at my own peril, diverting adverse attention from them to me. Nor should Karl require help authenticating stamps found at the Lünersee site. After all, they were once a part of his collection, or at least some of them were!

Could it be that the stamps were but a decoy and not Karl's chief agenda? Perhaps the Amber Room or gold bars, jewelry, coins, or other Nazi treasures are his primary focus? I knew without a doubt that gold and jewelry would be Mindy Slutkowski's motivation.

My concern increased as I studied the brochure outlining their honeymoon trip. The cruise included a three day tour of Austria, ample time for the Slarls to slip away and head over the ridge to the Lake Region and back. The Lünersee is a crater lake with an altitude of about 2000m, encircled by dramatic jagged, snow-covered peaks.

There is ample snow at that height to last throughout the year, making an exploration of the area even more challenging. If their intent was to linger for several days, they could connect with the ship at another port. The good news, according to the ship's itinerary, was that they weren't scheduled to be in Austria for another week.

If I hurried...

Chapter 5

It was midday. The Slarls sat on deck cuddling in their deckchairs. Mrs. Slarl, aka slut-woman, cooed,

"I love you so much, *Puddy Tat*! At last we're alone and don't have to worry about Edna or Elyse or whatever her stupid name is. Wonder what she's doing now, now that you're all mine. She'll never come between us again, will she?"

And she held out her hand to admire the huge dazzling rock and wedding band firmly ensconced on her sticky finger. Her other hand clutched a shot of Wild Turkey, an all too frequent companion. Karl patted her bleached head and grunted a reply, his thoughts elsewhere,

"I need an excuse to go ashore. I need to begin searching for the stamps that I and father had reburied several years ago once we reach the Austrian port. I doubt that anyone will follow. Elyse, as she likes to be called, has attracted enough international attention so that the focus of anyone else interested in the stamps will be upon her rather than me, or us—just as I have planned."

"What? What did you say?" Mindy queried. "You've got to speak up."

It was a shrewd guess that Karl would not be opposed to taking his new bride with him on the stamp search. If he did, his concern was for distracting her for a few hours while completing his quest. Perhaps they would find some touristy shops nearby to entertain and occupy her while he hiked into the site alone.

He would never reveal or share the true enormous value of the stamps with anyone, his new wife in particular. Mindy wasn't the brightest bulb in the chandelier. If she weren't foolish enough to use the stamps as letter postage, that crazy woman would resort to selling them to a pond shop or on eBay. Elyse could imagine her spending the money in its entirety on an extravaganza to Walmart.

Despite some reservations Karl might have, it is true that the *Slarl* union wasn't all for naught. Karl once commented that Mindy kept him warm at night—and, oh, so much more. From his descriptions, slut-woman was far more adventurous in the sack than were his previous wives.

This was pretty interesting information considering she was just a *li'l ol' Christian girl* from the south. A more apt description would be a *spicy chic-filet* from wherever.

The gentle motion of the boat soon worked its magic. The Slarls succumbed to the soothing lap of the waves and warmth of the sun, dozing off to their respective musings. They did not observe the figure in the shadow of the bridge scrutinizing them before gliding past.

Chapter 6

My last water voyage was a weekender to the Bahamas. While I had a most pleasant time, vacationing on a cruise ship has not been my favorite way to explore the world. There are a limited number of onboard entertainment options. Unless one is interested in spending each day sleeping, eating, exercising, or shopping, the time wears.

I'm far too restless to enjoy the confinement and much too independent to participate in group activities. Nor do I tolerate well, when ashore, being herded along with the rest of a large assemblage from one cold, sterile church to another.

On the positive side, it was wonderful having every need catered to. The variety and quality of food was excellent and available almost around the clock.

Traveling as a journalist has certain advantages. The crew is particularly accommodating, if you can convince everyone that you are writing a review of your cruise experiences for a new on-line magazine.

And, yes, for once, my cabin was above the water line. I could actually see the light of day! Are those porpoises performing acrobatic stunts in the distance? Wait, I forgot. This is a river cruise. The porthole in my suite provided an excellent view. I could enjoy the crystalline sky, expanse of water, and diverse shore lines without having to venture on deck.

There was little need to risk exposure to the Slarls or any other unsavory characters. Cruise passengers have sometimes disappeared under mysterious circumstances. Becoming such a statistic held little appeal.

Internet access was excellent, thanks to satellites hovering overhead. When the ship reached a port, tours were optional, so there would be ample time between working on Arturo's assignments, researching and eating, to ponder a most exceptional and *recent* clue.

Chapter 7

The evidence was concealed among a pile of mail that I had been sorting. This had occurred just before my departure to Budapest, where I had made arrangements to board the river cruise boat. It must have been in my box along with the usual array of bills and promotions.

The envelope stood in sharp contrast to the others more conventionally addressed. It bore in huge, bold letters, the script, *Addressee Unknown: Return to Sender*.

Since there *was* no return address, that seemed an impractical suggestion. The stamp the envelope bore was unusual as well. It resembled a map with a superimposed gray and white sketch of a cross bow.

After waging a brief skirmish with my conscience, thinking that maybe the mail had been intended for someone else, I pealed open the envelope. Its contents were little more than a copy of a very old black and white photograph. The photo showed three German officers standing outside the gates of what appeared to be one of the infamous WWII prison camps.

Their arms were linked and their expressions smug. They had posed against a background of obvious human suffering and death. Yet they looked carefree—like best buddies sharing a delightful secret or outing. Each looked as self-satisfied as the *cat that swallowed the canary*. In the photo's corner were penciled-in numbers.

On the back were scrawled the same three sets of numbers. The data were written in the manner of coordinates. Feeling that the information could be significant to my quest, I became determined to crack the code.

As I contemplated the picture, I wondered who on this ship might lend a helping hand determining the identity of the coordinates. Perhaps the ticket was to become friendly with one of the ship's officers. The coordinates could provide the perfect opening for a little recreational flirting as well as tapping into a useful information source.

An occasion arose much sooner than anticipated. Seated for dinner at my designated table, on my right, was one of the ship's officers. If this were someone's idea of match making, let the games begin. Not only was he cute, he turned out to be the navigator!

Chapter 8

Always a little shy around strangers, I lingered over a bourbon cocktail before attempting conversation. As long as liquor is mixed with a substantial amount of fruit juice, the taste and the effects are tolerable.

Of late, however, my interest in sampling cocktails had been stimulated by having attended the *Annual Whiskey Rebellion Dinner* in a town in southwestern PA, the actual site where the historical related events had unfolded.

At this annual commemoration of the rebellion, the mysteries of bourbon and scotch were compared, contrasted, and extolled. Then, there commenced a lively debate between the representatives of each of these beverage industries as to which of the products was superior.

A beautiful, articulate woman from Kentucky where the potion was brewed represented bourbon. The scotch representative was straight from the homeland. His brogue, rugged good looks, and the wearing of a kilt authenticated his heritage.

Each representative was prolific with information about their product. For instance, did you know that there are more barrels of bourbon in Kentucky than people? Or that Pennsylvania was the largest consumer of bourbon among all the states? Pennsylvania, I do believe, has Pittsburgh to thank for this dubious recognition.

Hardy Pittsburgh steel workers made the *Boilermaker* popular back in the city's steel heyday. The drink consists of beer with a shot of whiskey, *bourbon*, poured in for an extra kick. The beverage soon became the local favorite of that rugged then-industrial city. Its fame spread far and wide.

The cruise guests at the table seemed to enjoy sharing my new-found knowledge of scotch and bourbon. The quaint facts fascinated and amused them. As I spoke, I scanned the room, looking for familiar faces—other than those of Karl and slut-woman,

"During the bourbon refinement process an initial amount of bourbon is lost. This evaporated alcohol is referred to as the *Angel's Share*. Also, the oak barrels absorb a certain amount of the alcohol during the maturation process. This portion is reclaimed by agitating water in the barrel and then allowing it to set until the mix is more concentrated. The mixture, with its rich woody flavors, is referred to as the *Devil's Cut.*"

I paused for dramatic effect,

"Now, scotch made from malt can only be prepared in Scotland. Similar whiskey made in Canada, by law, must be referred to as Canadian whiskey, not scotch. Scotch has a burned woody flavor which is obscured by the alcohol."

I concluded by describing a method for detecting this smoky essence,

"You need only to splash a very small amount of the scotch onto your hands and then rub them together to evaporate the alcohol. After doing this, when you sniff your hands, the charred woody aroma is quite strong."

The other guests at the table, interests piqued and thirsts stimulated by my explanations, ordered a round of drinks or shots.

Perhaps I should be on commission.

My cocktail-induced, relaxed state reversed itself when I noticed the Slarls at a table not too far from mine. The animated chatter of our group stood in sharp contrast to the awkward silence at some of the other tables, theirs in particular. They were too busy necking, to the consternation of those seated with them.

To deal with the situation, I averted my face and leaned back far enough in my chair to obscure myself from their line of vision... and them from mine. Though too polite to say anything, Neal, the ship's navigator, regarded my awkward posture with puzzlement.

Despite the gracelessness of the situation, we continued to converse:

"Tell me," I said, reclining 45 degrees from the side of my chair. My head was turned at a most uncomfortable angle to look at him,

"How do you manage to navigate the buoys and currents? And how can you tell when you're off course?"

When Neal's eyes lit up, I could tell it was a subject near and dear to his heart. I listened to his explanations of plotting, then following, coordinates,

"Of course, everything now is computerized. But in the rare event of a computer failure, it's wise to be familiar with the old ways, which at one time were passed from generation to generation. Not so much now since people have come to be dependent on GPS systems."

We then made arrangements to meet on deck after dinner, where he would share with me the mysteries of night navigation... and who knows what else...

Chapter 9

I scurried back to my cabin to change, wishing I had packed something more seductive. I pondered while walking, *if I were something sexy, what would I be?* Just after I had reached my cabin, as if on cue, Karl and his new bride sauntered past my open porthole.

Speaking of sexy, her push up-and-out-and-over bra enhanced her cleavage to the extent that her ample breasts spilled over the neckline of her leopard-print sweater. Averting my head, I dropped to the floor lest I be noticed and recognized should they glance through my porthole. I could still hear slut-woman bellowing,

"I tell you, that woman looked just like your friend Ethel (one of my aliases). Did you see her monopolizing conversation at her table during dinner? Of all the nerve... her being here during our honeymoon... Getting her out of our hair can't happen quickly enough."

Karl admonished,

"Shush, she won't be a problem for long. We don't want everyone, or anyone, to become suspicious of our plans for..." Their voices trailed off as they moved further down the deck past my porthole."

What a curious conversation. It was the kind that, when overheard, puts a damper on one's evening plans. It sounded as though they, or someone, had been hired to... well, it was too frightening to contemplate.

Could they have been referring to me? Geez! What the heck.

Were they discussing the elimination of another living human being... probably me? Mindy Slutkowski was speaking in the same loud, but unexcited tones she would use to recite a jewelry or liquor list.

Who else could they be referring to?

"Well!" I thought rallying, "Two—three—can play this game!"

I flaunted my fearlessness by jumping into my bunk and pulling the comforter over my head to satiate my sudden need for security. I began to mutter,

"If I wanted to dissuade someone from being successful, there are options other than disfigurement or death. There is distraction."

In fact, distraction may be the explanation for why I have been lured all over the globe: induced to touch down in so many different locations. These were places I would never have visited or revisited under normal circumstances. This quest has taken me nearly everywhere—everywhere but Austria, my ultimate destination.

Perhaps, because I remained persistent in my pursuit of the stamps, Plan A, which consisted of distraction, had been deemed ineffective. Now, the villains in this play are scrapping Plan A and implementing the alternative. Plan B seems to include reducing the population count by one—me.

This ship could provide, should the Slarls or the assassin find and recognize me, the perfect opportunity for elimination. Such a simple matter it would be—disposing of a body in the secretive waters of the swiftly moving river!

Was I drafted for this quest merely to flush out the competition? If Karl were successful in identifying and eliminating his enemies from *Odessa* or the *DKDKD*, perhaps he felt that now I was nothing more than another loose end. Therefore, he was moving from Plan A to Plan B, which involved D and/or F (Death and/or disfigurement)? He seems to have skipped Plan C.

My list of assassin suspects included Greg, the Mt. Washington, NH meteorologist. At the time, I had been suspicious of his Germanic accent and tattoo. Who else in the group might have had tattoos and German or Austrian accents, and a blood lust? It could have been any one of the Scandinavian *Nameless* members who had joined my quest. Because of the season and climates, their arms were constantly covered with long-sleeve bulky sweaters.

This Scandinavian connection had been recommended to me by my US contacts in the organization *Nameless*, a spin-off of Anonymous. They had diverted me from Austria to Amsterdam, to Sweden, and finally to Newfoundland before returning to the states.

Then there was Karl himself. He was proving to be as conniving and ruthless as any assassin. But, since he had referred to the dispatcher in the third person, it was unlikely that Karl was the hit man.

This situation called for a private moment with my laptop to once again research the significance of the various tattoo designs. I must determine if there was a connection between them and *Odessa*, or some weird treasure-worshipping religious cult, or perhaps another rogue corporation.

I needed to cease with the paranoia, but remain vigilant and cautious. It was evident that a few allies would be most welcome right now. Could I be regretting my decision to resume the quest without Arturo and Saul by my side?

****

Neal was waiting with a huge welcoming smile when at last I ventured to the ship's bridge, punctual for my appointment with the handsome navigator. His obvious eagerness made me feel as though I were the evening's designated dessert. After exchanging a few pleasantries, he scrutinized the coordinates I provided for his interpretation.

While he studied the coordinates, I inspected his rugged profile. It was close to perfect. Though, his brow was furrowed in concentration as he plotted each set of the mystery coordinates in a methodical manner. I admired his focus. Was there anything about this man not to like?

According to his analyses, the first coordinate set indicated a lake in Germany. This was a place where my latent scuba-diving skills may become useful. The second set did not point to a body of water, but, instead, to a terra firma location. The third set of coordinates supported a different area in Germany. Perhaps I would swing by and check out these other sites after I paid Lake Lünersee in Austria a thorough exploratory visit.

I accepted an invitation to meet Neal later for an evening stroll around the deck. With that activity to look forward to and armed with the coordinate information provided by him, I rushed back to my cabin I began plotting an efficient route to the various treasure sites.

Chapter 10

Although tales of Nazi treasures abound in Europe, the whereabouts of the vast majority of property stolen from Europe's Jews by the Nazis remains a mystery. It was an unusual occurrence for any of the few found treasures to be returned to the rightful owners.

A former CIA and US treasury official once projected that a mere one fifth of the wealth stolen from Europe during the Second World War and the Holocaust has been returned. This fact remained, despite numerous clear and explicit international agreements and country promises made during World War II and right after.

I felt confident that I could improve those statistics as I became more familiar with the disposal methods practiced by the Nazis. Their approach to treasure concealment seemed consistent and simplistic:

Dump it into lakes or toss it down a mine shaft, and then execute those who aided in the concealment. Oh, yeah, don't forget to booby trap the sight afterwards.

For now, clues of a most mysterious origin, my computer, and the charming navigation officer's course-plotting tools were the resources at hand for pinpointing several of those sites.

Coordinate Set #1 indicated a site near Hermann Goering's Carinhall and *Stolpsee* Lake. Why is Lake *Stolpsee* rated high on the treasure hunter's list? Hermann Goering's principle job was commander of the Luftwaffe until he was demoted to the role of acquisitioning the property and artwork of war victims. Goering accumulated astonishing wealth from the lands conquered by the Nazis and the dozens of rare masterpieces stolen from galleries across Europe.

Following the Nazi invasion in 1939, according to legend, Goering took charge of numerous amounts of bullion from the national bank of Poland, hiding it in his home.

Imagine hiding the entire contents of a bank in your home!

In 1945, fearful that the approaching Russian lines would loot his house, he emptied his country home, Carinhall, of all stolen gold, jewels, and art treasures. He then dynamited the structure to keep it from falling into the clutches of the Red Army towards the closing weeks of the war.

Goering used Polish prisoner slaves to dump the stolen gold worth a billion pounds in a German lake. After completing their thankless task, the slaves were riddled with machine gun fire. Their bodies were dumped into the lake's watery depths by the accompanying soldiers.

Over the years, many adventurers searched for the estimated 18 boxes of gold thrown into the 400 foot deep *Stolpsee* Lake. The area was, at that time a part of the post-war Communist East Germany.

In 1986 the East Germans conducted another unsuccessful search for the treasure. Their failure dampened enthusiasm for the quest. However, the claims of a local priest, Erich Koehler have, in recent years, reignited fervor for the search.

As Father Keebler, a gentle man in his late seventies, pointed out after researching the legend of the Carinhall Treasure,

> They didn't have the technology in the former East Germany to scrutinize all areas of the lake, but there are enough local people still around to know that the gold is there, as well as whatever remains of the poor souls who were forced to dump the gold into the water.
>
> I heard the tales when just a youngster. The villagers spoke about the atrocities committed by the Germans and the many treasures they stole and hid.
>
> Discovered SS documents, together with other post-war eyewitness statements to the events on the lake, gave credence to the old priest's claims. It is believed that precious material was indeed *dumped into the 400-feet deep lake in March 1945.*

Another witness, Eckhard Litz, revealed to a post-war allied commission,

> Even though just a youngster, I shall never forget the night that Lorries, with slit headlights, drove up to the lakeshore.
>
> About 20 to 30 of the skinniest men imaginable dressed in the striped clothing of concentration camp inmates were forced to unload heavy boxes, which they dropped into two row boats. How they had the strength to do this in their emaciated state is beyond me.
>
> These boats made several trips to the center of the lake. When the last case had been dumped overboard, the men were returned to shore and lined up. The last thing I saw were the flashes of the machine guns of the guards as they shot the inmates.
>
> The dead bodies were thrown into boats and taken to the middle of the lake where they were dumped. They then sank all the boats used to haul them. A third boat brought the SS Officers back to shore.

His story was almost identical to that of Father Keebler.

Many documents describing this and other unclaimed treasures still lie among the millions of papers in the Berlin archive of the Stasi (*Staatssicherheit*) secret police, once regarded as one of the most effective and repressive intelligence and secret police agencies in the world. To this day the ruins of Goering's Carinhall attract scores of treasure hunters each weekend.

What's one more, eh?

Although the likelihood that any treasures remain in such a well-combed area is negligible, there may be clues that have been long overlooked. It was worth a look. Besides, the excursion could be fun and provide some much needed camaraderie.

Coordinate Set #2 indicated another Alpine lake. What is it about treasures and lakes? It just so happens that the second set of coordinates was for Lake Toplitz, another Austrian Alpine lake and favorite dumping site of the Nazis. Some dream that the *Amber Room* was disassembled and stashed in this lake. Others speculate that it is gold that was hidden there. Bountiful rumors support both.

The world famous Amber Room was a most beautiful and recognizable piece of art—often referred to as the Eighth wonder of the World. In 1701, a Prussian King named Friedrich Wilhelm received a gift made from Amber. Overwhelmed with its appearance, he ordered a master Amber artist to create a giant wall covering made entirely from that same substance.

The 16-foot jigsaw-puzzle style panels were constructed of more than 100,000 perfectly fitted pieces of amber, containing six tons of the precious resin and requiring 10 years for some of Europe's finest craftsmen to complete. The resulting room was a magnificent baroque masterpiece, comprised of three tiers.

The middle tier contained exquisite murals and the lower tier was structured with squares of amber. When candles were lit, it was a study of ethereal and brilliant beauty.

The masterpiece passed through a number of royal hands by the time it reached Tsar Peter the Great in St. Petersburg. Eighteen horse-drawn wagons brought this present from the King of Prussia to St. Petersburg in 1716 in an effort to cement a military alliance against the Swedes.

The room was first erected in the Tsar's Winter Palace in St. Petersburg. In 1755, after having a new generation of craftsmen embellish the room, Catherine the Great had the panels moved from the Winter Palace in St. Petersburg to her new Summer Palace at Tsarkoe Selo, 17 miles south of the Imperial Russian capital.

In 1941, when the German army surrounded Leningrad, they occupied Tsarkoe Selo in addition to other outlying areas. The Nazis did not overlook the Amber Room when plundering. Under the supervision of Sommes Laubach, the German "Art Protection" officer, they packed the precious panels into 27 crates. Laubach's qualification for supervising the room's transport was no more than the equivalent of a Bachelor's degree in art history.

They shipped the crates to Germany. There they reassembled and then displayed the glorious panels in the

Castle of Konigsberg, along with other treasures looted by them during this period. In August 1944, after Allied bombing efforts, the castle lay in ruins, but the Amber room had vanished.

Theories concerning the priceless room's disappearance abound. One notion is that the Germans melted down the panels. Another suggests that they were destroyed during the ferocious Red Army attack on the East Prussian city of Konigsberg where the Germans had stored them.

Yet another theory conjectures that a Nazi ship that was torpedoed by the Russians had been transporting them in the Baltic. In 2003, a TV documentary in Germany suggested the room, worth 120 million at today's prices, was abandoned in a mine in the former East Germany.

Chapter 11

Theories and legends flourish, but as of yet remain unsubstantiated. Treasure hunters swear to the existence of documentation proving that the Amber room was packed up and hidden away. Tests of the castle ruins showed no signs of Amber fragments, supporting the premise that the panels were not destroyed in the castle.

Surfacing clues suggest that this amazing piece of history still remains, somewhere, waiting to be found. One rumor supports the claim that the coordinates for the room's hiding place are stamped on the amber seal, one of the amber room's panels.

Unless the stamped panel is hidden separately, away from the other panels, this information is useless as a clue.

The vanished Amber Room has become the new El Dorado, the pot at the end of a rainbow, a quixotic quest, captivating the imagination of the wealthy and the poor alike.

Recent explorations include a team of treasure hunters intending to search the entire bottom of Lake Toplitz. It is 338 feet deep and situated in the heart of Austria.

I pondered this information. Once a skilled scuba diver myself, perhaps if I hurried I could charm my way into becoming a part of the team. At the very least, I could serve as chief cook and bottle washer for the explorers.

The adventure may not end in unimaginable wealth. But it could be the source of another good article for Arturo's magazine, entitled: *Secrets Lurk in Liquid Murk.*

The adventurers planned to energize the search by using sonar, robots, and unmanned submarines. Such equipment would allow for more underwater time, as well as minimizing harm to the lake while curtailing human loss.

These same treasure hunters were searching for Nazi gold. That is, until a conjecture that the Amber Room might also be in the lake diverted their attention,

The Amber Room went somewhere and research shows railway links with Konigsberger (now the Russian city of Kaliningrad) to Lake Toplitz. This means that it could have been transported there within three to four days, despite communications disruptions caused by Allied bombing.

A local unnamed witness counted 27 crates being dumped into the waters of the lake in April 1945, one month before the capitulation of Nazi Germany. Records kept by the RHSA—the Reich Main Security Office of the SS in wartime—verifies that the Amber Room was packed into 27 crates before being carted away by the Germans.

They found the remains of a wooden crate in the lake. Written on its side is what they think are the words *fragile* in Cyrillic lettering, along with a number. Perhaps this crate once contained a piece of the Amber Room jigsaw.

But the Cyrillic inscription on the crate is difficult to interpret. The letters are not standard Cyrillic, but some distortion of it.

By using the odd lettering, perhaps the Russians prisoners forced to pack and ship the room were providing a clue! Accessing a photo taken of the odd lettering, if not the actual crate, would facilitate solving the puzzle.

Evidence that the crates may have deteriorated gave me cause for concern. Would the lack of protection affect the quality of the Amber Room panels? Would they begin to deteriorate, perhaps dissolve, after a prolonged period of underwater exposure?

Many have said that the lake often does take on a golden hue. Old timers share that, sometimes, mist seen rising from the lake has the appearance of opaque yellowish tendrils.

According to experts, true amber does not dissolve in plain water. But, a boiling solution of fixed alkali will dissolve it. The alkali bonds with the amber to form a kind of soap that is soluble in alcohol or water.

Diluted acids have no effect on amber, but an alcoholic solution of potash dissolves 40-55% of it. So does high-test gasoline.

Chapter 12

I looked at the time. I had another hour before I needed to meet Neal. So speculate on, I say.

I was concerned. Hitler's forces used Lake Toplitz in the last two years of the war for secret underwater experiments involving dynamite and rockets. Deterioration of the amber was a legitimate cause for anxiety.

And if explosive experiments weren't enough, the Nazis later turned the lake into a dumping ground. They used it to conceal anything they wanted to hide from the advancing Allies.

If more crate remains, but no amber, were found, the odds for the panels having survived were low. At the rate Germans were dumping and exploding material in the lake, one speculates that they created a water pH that minimized the survival of any exposed amber.

This was a prospect too terrible for treasure hunters, for Mother Russia, who sorely missed the opulent splendor, and for me to contemplate. One could hope, of course, that the Nazis had concealed the amber elsewhere.

While some accounts have the crates being discarded into the lake, others claim to be eye-witnesses to them being dropped down a mine shaft.

Whatever!

Always a pragmatic person, I decided to expand my very narrow focus on stamps and the Amber Room to an all-treasure inclusive. I would head anywhere, anytime I get a hot lead, but only after concluding my primary quest—the Lünersee stamp collection.

I made a quick series of phone calls. At last I made personal contact with a few of the better known treasure hunters.

They confided their confidence that the Germans had moved the Amber Room to Austria and then dumped it into the lake to hide evidence of Nazi looting. A spokesman for the US treasure hunters said, "We've put two and two together and have come up with a convincing argument for what we believe is the Amber Room that lies down there.

Why else would the Nazis declare that area to be a top security zone?"

Why else indeed?

They also informed me that diving in the lake requires special permission from the authorities. The few official dives that have taken place have unearthed little more than war relics, including the counterfeit UK currency, and, listen closely, *false stamps*, dynamite, weapons, fake British currency and other memorabilia. The fraudulent bank notes were to be used to undermine the British economy.

False stamps!

My scalp prickled and goose bumps surfaced! Hadn't we previously speculated that the Lünersee stamps could be disguised to appear as fake stamps? Well, why not false stamps?

A scientific team had also discovered a hitherto unknown anaerobic worm. That knowledge could be useful to a fish species that also survived in the oxygen-deprived water.

But, again, Lake Toplitz is not the only suspected site for the Amber Room treasure. A German team digging at a site in Deutschneudorf in February of 2008 claimed to have found the room, in addition to two tons of Nazi gold. Then with no explanation, all digging stopped.

Communication leaks from the treasure hunters' camp revealed that digging ceased when it was feared that the shaft might collapse, setting off booby traps.

One of the treasure hunter's fathers was a navigator in the Luftwaffe. Before he died, *in a most mysterious fashion* I might add, he had confided in a farewell note that he had helped hide the gold and treasures when the Nazis realized they were losing the war.

Equipment used to pinpoint treasure at the site reacted as it would if it had located precious metals that can only be gold or silver. Other metal, like copper, would not have set the instruments off.

The electromagnetic pulse measurements taken in the man-made chamber 20 meters underground near the village of Deutschneudorf led the team to believe that the cavern contains gold. An anonymous collaborator, who has been seeking the Amber Room in the Ore Mountain region for a decade said that he is 90% sure they have found the gold, and, perhaps, the Amber Room.

So, perhaps, there are two Amber Rooms, or the panels had been hidden in two different places, or someone is exaggerating, or lying.

I glanced at the clock and decided to change. I applied a little makeup, lip gloss and eye shadow, to prepare for my rendezvous with Neal.

Just then, the phone rang. It was my date, pushing our time back by yet another hour.

Excellent, more time to explore information relating to the clues.

Once again, the present merged with the past. While speculation and excavation concerning the Amber room and other clues continue, Russia, at least, has had some good fortune.

Treasures stolen from one of the Russian museums by the Nazis have found their way back home. Two crates with hundreds of rare exhibits that were stolen in 1941 were *voluntarily*, if not eagerly, returned to Russia by a Wehrmacht doctor's son.

Rumor has it that at the time he had made the decision to return the ill-gotten gains of his father, he was under the amorous influence of a well-endowed Ukrainian Pyrohy, *dumpling,* whose methods of persuasion were far less traumatic and more tantalizing than water boarding and electroshock.

A mental image of slut-woman pervaded my thoughts. I remain unconvinced that she is the naïve li'l ol' Christian chic from the south that she represents herself to be.

If it were she, her powers of persuasion are inarguable.

She had Karl under her spell. He was consumed with her, following her about like a lost puppy.

****

A museum in the city of Tver, located north of Moscow, received the treasure. The unexpected parcel contained 480

Janet Feduska Cole

objects, including a collection of crosses, archeological findings and icons. To the astonishment of the museum employees, many of the objects returned were items of extreme rarity and value.

Chapter 13

The counterfeit foreign currency that kept popping up in Lake Toplitz was quite a different story. Many historians believe it to be related to Operation Bernhard, another top secret German project.

The idea for the operation had come from Hitler himself! Skilled printers were recruited from concentration camps, located in a centralized camp and provided the best printing and graphic equipment available. Their mission was to counterfeit enemy currency to use as payment towards the war effort, while weakening the enemies' economies.

Operation Bernhard resulted in the counterfeiting of the equivalent of $4.5 billion pounds, mostly British. This process distressed the bank of England, which, after the war, recalled and redesigned all its currency. The project also targeted the American dollar, but the war ended before any significant amount of United States currency was placed in circulation.

When operation Bernhard was moved out of Berlin, the SS chose to hide the evidence at the bottom of Lake Toplitz. Where else? When in doubt, dump it in a lake.

Ahh, what else lurked in those watery depths?

In 1963, a German sport diver was hired to find out, but died during the attempt. His unlucky "accident" reeked of *Odessa*. He was later found wedged among rocks with his air hose slashed. Authorities claimed that the anaerobic worm ate through the hose.

Really?

The Austrian government responded to the tragedy by making it illegal to dive in the lake for the purpose of hunting treasure, much to remaining *Odessa* members' delight, since their goal was to protect the treasures that were required to finance the *Rise Again* movement.

The Austrian government initiated a search of its own. The operation located more crates of counterfeit money on the bottom along with the printing plates needed to make forgeries. Rockets, projectiles, mines and other experimental weapons were also salvaged. During the war, the Germans tested torpedoes in Toplitz, including a missile that could be launched by a submarine from underwater.

By 1983 the popular belief was that the lake had surely been cleansed of all Nazi material. For Lake Toplitz, it was the "Year of the Worm."

In 1983, Professor Hans Flickle, started diving in Toplitz. He had obtained special permission to dive to research what kind of life might survive in the lake's oxygen-deprived depths. It was his scientific team that discovered the hose-eating worm.

They also discovered several types of bacteria and possible clues to the whereabouts of the Amber Room. But Fricke never came across anything else of value.

Ask yourselves, would he admit to it if he had? That Amber Room could finance for him many research projects.

My confusion lay in trying to figure out what the oxygen-less worm ate—besides hoses, that is.

There be slim culinary pickings' in such a lake, even for a worm. Hope it doesn't like stamps!

The most complete examination of the lake came in the year 2000. A company named SeaFaring Technologies searched the lake bottom inch-by-inch using a remote-controlled submarine.

They found the lake floor littered with trees knocked into the lake from the surrounding mountains, the result of avalanches. In some places the lake floor was stacked with as much as 60 feet of wood.

Using the submarine in this type of environment was difficult and dangerous. Its long tether connected it to the crew on the surface. The tether was always in danger of becoming entangled in the dead branches and roots on the floor of the lake.

When the robot submarine found what appeared to be the remains of a crate, SeaFaring sent down a manned submarine. They found more forged British bank notes and more *false stamps*, but no Amber Room, or gold bars, or stamps.

My stamp sensor had gone off.

Stamps! Did someone say stamps? Someone had found stamps... in a lake? False stamps?

I'm familiar with *fake* stamps, but what in bloody hell were *false* stamps? Were these stamps used during Nazi spy missions into Great Britain?

Were they the false stamps manufactured by French prisoners during WWI? Or, could they be the Lünersee stamps, whose appearance had been *faked* to look like *false* stamps to further conceal their identity.

I put in a call for the Fraud Squad team, Jürgen and Walder. Could the Lünersee stamps have been dropped into Lake Toplitz and not Lake Lünersee? I needed to find and examine said stamps, particularly if I found none during my search at Lünersee.

What other discoveries *unofficial* dives had rendered was anybody's guess. Security at the lake was lax and authorities admitted that there was no way of telling how many unauthorized treasure dives had taken place there.

Several individuals paid with their lives in the search for Nazi bounty in the oxygen-deprived depths of Lake Toplitz.

Alfred Eger, 19, was the first to die after being hired by former SS officers to explore the depths of the lake in 1963. His mission was to search for watertight tubes. These tubes, they believed, contained the numbers to Nazi Swiss bank accounts that held more loot from conquered lands.

Consider the character of his employers. It could be that Alfred, the nineteen year old diver, had discovered the tubes holding the Swiss bank Nazi account numbers.

I conjecture that, after the tubes' discovery, the Nazis *arranged* Alfred's death, sending him back into the watery depths for all eternity to prevent details of their discovery from becoming public! Perhaps, the tubes weren't all that he found.

This next Toplitz story oozes of horror and suspense! It describes the supposed bloody demise of four divers,

> Hoping to swim about a little to get a feel for what else might have been hidden in the artefact-laden lake, this particular group of adventurers donned their scuba gear. They performed the prescribed backward somersault off

the boat. After they were under the surface for but a few moments, a pool of frothy blood seeped up from where they had entered the water.

Their bodies were never reclaimed, giving rise to the myth of the Toplitz Two-horned Demon. This monster satisfied its cravings by devouring unsuspecting treasure-hunters.

Perhaps it was a fervent *Odessa* member who came up with that story, hoping to discourage other treasure seekers.

Or, perhaps the two-horned monster was a member of the *DKDKD*, the secret society of renegade philatelists. Members of this group were determined to acquire stamps, *false* or otherwise, at any cost.

Or, perhaps the mutant anaerobic worm, a lone creature in the murky waters had sharp teeth. Perhaps this lonely and ravenous worm discovered that there were more than just air hoses to savour and feast upon.

Chapter 14

While treasure hunters continued their search for the Amber Room, in 1979, a *reconstruction* effort of the amber room began at *Tsarkoe Selo*, using black and white photographs of the original Amber Room, taken before the Nazis dismantled it.

The restoration team completed the simulation in 2003. Russian President Vladimir Putin and German Chancellor Gerhard Schroeder opened the restored room in time for the 300-year anniversary of St. Petersburg (previously Leningrad).

My suspicions were aroused upon learning that, under Austrian law, the profits from all recovered WWII artefacts are to be divided between the Austrian government and the company or individual recovering them. When appropriate, a portion of the rewards would go to the Jewish Federation.

If ownership is determined, the Austrian government forfeits its profit to the heirs. The heirs then must negotiate discovery fees with the party having recovered the treasure.

Such huge claims on recovered treasures may have been incentive for the Germans to conceal their discovery of amber-laden crates from all but the Russians. Perhaps they secretly returned the Amber room to the Russians upon negotiating a reward far greater than would be available if sharing the treasure with the Austrian government.

Perhaps the *new* Amber Room was actually a *reassembly* rather than duplication. The fact that the new room is not as ornate as the original could indicate that they had not located all the crates containing the amber pieces. Perhaps the panels had been hidden in Lake Toplitz and Deutschneudorf.

Third Set of Coordinates: The charming Navigation Officer had also plotted for me the third set of coordinates. Perhaps my research of these would have to wait until after my date.

I looked again at the clock. Although I was growing weary and hungry while awaiting the call from Neal, I explored information relating to the third set of coordinates.

This activity kept me from fretting over the possibility of having been stood up.

The coordinate information was hand-scrawled on the picture concealed among the rest of my mail. The envelope itself was plenty weird. The postal phrase, *Addressee Unknown: Return to Sender,* was stamped on the envelope in place of an address. And, yet, someone had placed it in *my* box. There was no return address, so how could I *Return to Sender*?

The navigation officer had identified the third set of coordinates as the location of Biro Chateau in the former Czech Republic. Experts found a false bottom in the well where a Nazi treasure was allegedly hidden.

War survivors mentioned the existence of the false bottom, and historical sources claimed that there is a secret medieval passage from the castle to the well's bottom where members of the Nazi staff stashed stolen valuable items.

Explorers uncovered Nazi documents from the recesses of the well. In addition to the documents, 20 weapons were uncovered. The excavation has been on-going for more than a year. Some documents unearthed from the National Archives state,

> We know from witnesses that a Nazi aircraft landed and large cases were unloaded and taken to the castle. We know that the last SS fled on foot without their uniforms and without taking anything. No one has found any trace of the cases and no one knows what was in them. The castle has a series of tunnels and secret passages that were closed off behind cement walls erected by the Nazis.

The great fear is that the well is booby trapped with explosives. So to this day those secret passages remain unexplored. This sounds like the same site where exploration ceased just a few short years ago for the very same reasons.

What happened to having an intrepid spirit like that of the buccaneers who once trolled the high seas? They feared nothing! We'll have to change this scaredy-cat image, won't we?

Again, I pondered the reality that treasure team searches were inconclusive because of the hazard presented by explosives and cave-ins. There are risk takers in every group, and treasure hunters were in general a fearless lot, enjoying life on the edge. And now there was technology.

If Lake Toplitz could be explored with robots and remotely-operated mechanical devices, couldn't this technology be transferable to mine shafts and tunnels. Could not robots explore those shafts in a manner similar to that used in the lake?

If exploration efforts detonated the explosives, then only *R2D2 and* his robotic associates would have met their demise. Our loss would be financial; it would not affect life and limb. Of course, a free-thinking robot, in a moment of panic, or sheer rebellion, could hurl an explosive up the shaft entrance to save itself as well as rid itself of its controllers.

Chapter 15

Neal had called once again, bumping our date back by yet another hour. I was reconciling myself to the fact that I had been stood up. That embarrassing fact was no longer speculation. So I did what any jilted cruise date would do. I wallowed in other Treasure Tales.

Quite frankly, I was pissed!

What was going on? Was he another player—one of these guys who juggled several women, arranging consecutive dates with different people on the same night, *making hay* while the sun shines? Oh well. I decided to just play along. Our friendship was transitory at best.

My favorite WWII organization has always been MI5. I had read several books regarding MI5's decryption and encryption efforts during the war. Through their many successful decoding efforts, in 1943, MI5 uncovered a Nazi plot to smuggle gold to Argentina in 1943.

According to secret messages and files, Nazi leaders were planning to traffic plundered jewelry and gold in a submarine. The details of this mission emerged from MI5's interrogation of Ernesto Hoppe, an agent of the German Intelligence service, as a result of intercepted coded messages.

MI5 arrested Hoppe, code name of Herold, *Herry Hoppe aka Fuzzy Bunny*, in Gibraltar in 1943. The British agents took him to MI5's interrogation center where they forced him to consume an excess of scones and tea. They refused him bathroom privileges until he confessed.

Under the described duress, he claimed that he had been approached by a German Luftwaffe colonel. The Nazis outlined for him a plan for a quick exit to Argentina if the Third Reich were defeated. The U-boat cargo was to be their little secret 401k retirement fund.

So many secret stashes existed. How did they keep track! Perhaps I have hit the nail on the head. They didn't keep accurate track and therein lay the explanation for reclamation of only 20% of all Nazi stolen treasures.

Other governments have long accused Argentina's central bank of holding Nazi gold after WWII. It has been no secret that many Nazis fled to Argentina. Once there, they were given a warm and fuzzy welcome with open arms. The quantity of gold the Nazis delivered there remains a mystery.

Researchers investigating Nazi activities in Argentina obtained a letter signed by a former Argentinian foreign minister. In the letter, dated as 1946, he requested that the gold be deposited in the bank. Prior to that time, the Swiss embassy in Buenos Aires held the money for the Germans.

The research coordinator of the commission of inquiry on Nazi activities in Argentina, stated,

"For the first time, we have evidence that Argentina was the recipient of Nazi gold *and stamps*."

Finding proof that the looted gold was part of a money-laundering operation would bring Argentina one step closer to making reparations to the many victims.

Ahh, Argentina, Argentina... During the 1940s, the country was a veritable hotbed of Nazis hiding their stolen wealth and seeking political refuge! It was in that country that Karl acquired his most auspicious and suspicious stamp collection. His suspected source was the evil Dr. Mengele, the *Angel of Death*, of concentration camp infamy.

Chapter 16

The word or two that pops into one's mind when pondering the Nazis' motivation for plundering the treasures of others are *ruthlessness* and *greed*! Not only did the Nazis raid museums of their assets, they also took families' possessions.

Hitler's methodical process of plundering the nations he invaded was multi-purposed: 1) He needed to fund his war machine. 2) He was a lover of art despite being a failed art student. Possessing art by the world's masters was a thrill beyond comprehension for him. 3) He sought to destroy a nation's historicity in addition to its economy. Not only would he bring the country to its financial knees, he would destroy its identity.

Once a country lost its distinctiveness, after a generation or two with most traces of the past erased, that country was more likely to accept its new masters.

Despite the tales of plunder and gold floating about, the Dachau Lünersee stamp treasure continued to hold me under its spell. In addition to the stamps I sought, the Dachau treasure included jewels and gold. The plunder had belonged to about 35,000 Jewish prisoners before they were thrown into that ignominious concentration camp during the years of 1933 through 1945.

Once again, legend placed the burial of this treasure in the vicinity of the Austrian Alpine Lake Lünersee. After reclaiming the Lünersee stamps and satisfying my curiosity regarding the Amber Room, I intended to immerse myself in the treasure hunting scene.

I proposed the use of robots in booby-trapped mines, such as the one in Deutschneudorf. If they get blown to smithereens because, well, the mine *was* booby-trapped, then, at least, the explosives would no longer be a worry.

My eyes do begin to tear up as I think of all the little robots who would never again venture into a cave or mine shaft. Their little blinking lights and rapid-toned communications would become nothing more than a memory, as will Karl and S-woman if I were able to get my hands on them. Perhaps I would add Neal to that list, I thought, with a sudden surge of hostility.

Tum tee dum...

The Honor ring treasure, although interesting, held little fascination for me. Perhaps it was because the information was vague. Perhaps it was because I had not heard any emotion-laced stories of someone winning the ring through an act of extraordinary valor. Perhaps it was because they belonged to the enemy.

SS Honor rings where given to Nazi soldiers who showed bravery in the field of duty. The 14,500 sterling silver rings were manufactured in Munich. When the soldier wearing it died in battle, the ring was to be returned.

By the end of the war, 9,280 rings were returned to the castle. According to that count, less than 5000 of the original ring recipients survived. An SS soldier was later ordered to hide these rings in a cave, destroying the entrance.

To this day the majority of the jewelry remains lost. A few have been found in the fields of battle or were passed down through families.

The authentic SS Honor ring is worth up to $12,000 in today's market. However, the discovery of all the rings would decrease the estimated value.

Imagine finding 9,000 of these SS ornaments, if each were valued at $6,000. In total you would have $54,000,000. *Not too shabby a find.* I decided that I would leave the solution of this mystery to others—rings make my fingers itch.

Chapter 17

Still no call from Neal!
A show of hands from those familiar with the location of the Auckland Islands! I could envision Saul and Arturo both raising their hands. Initially, I confused the Auckland Islands with the Falkland Islands.

Turns out the Auklands are near New Zealand. The Falkland Islands are near Argentina. You may ask, why such an interest in these remote, isolated bodies of land? Reading the words treasure and Auckland islands in the same sentence motivated me to pull out my trusty globe and atlas.

The largest of New Zealand's sub-Antarctic islands is approximately 625 sq. km., or 241.3 sq. miles. The Nazis knew where the islands were. Their U-Boats visited them. Towards the end of the war, some speculate that the Nazis went there to hide boxes of gold, silver and foreign currency. It is not known whether they buried the boxes on the island. Perhaps the soldiers sunk the treasures in a specific off-shore site.

Rumours that the Germans had stashed gold at sea more than 50 years ago may have been validated in the '90s. An individual traveling there insisted that he sighted two large objects on the seabed near the Auckland Islands,

"They didn't bring the objects all the way from Germany to stash it if the containers were full of old tin cans."

There is no real proof to substantiate this story. But the lookout towers on some of the islands give credence to speculation that they were used for a short time by Nazi soldiers. No doubt to guard something of value.

Each lost Nazi treasure is spectacular in its own way. Either it possesses unparalleled beauty and value, or it is remarkable because of the lore associated with it.

The fact remains—each treasure belongs to the people, not just one single person. The sources for most of the gold and silver bars were the coins, gold teeth, and jewelry of the imprisoned and condemned, melted down into bars.

Hitler's plan was to hide all such valuable and irreplaceable treasures. *If* he lost the war, he would have adequate funds to rebuild the Nazi regime.

His efforts were diffused and fragmented. His hard work resembled the industrious, but random, hiding of nuts engaged in every fall by squirrels.

Most of these treasures will remain undiscovered— unless discovered by accident.

Chapter 18

At last that elusive call came. Neal was apologetic. He claimed that the next officer on duty ran into a glitch, so was late getting to the bridge to relieve him

It was close to dusk when at last I was to embark on an intriguing evening with my handsome navigator friend. I must admit, because of the long wait, some of the romantic appeal had waned. The excursion, I decided, was just to be for rest and relaxation, with perhaps a little romance thrown into the mix.

I had worked hard and deserved a little break, eh?

I looked in the mirror and decided that my current outfit looked a little disheveled, after all the hours of poring over computer files. Returning to the closet, I pulled out a low-cut black silk tank top, black silk pants and black sandals, purchased earlier, during an onboard shopping spree.

The outfit was slinky, but not overstated. At least that is how the saleswoman had described it. It was perfect for someone attempting to appear seductive while maintaining a low profile.

I no longer cared about seduction. I just wanted *food* and a little company. After re-showering and re-blow-drying my hair, I dressed and then inspected myself in the full-length mirror.

Not half bad!

Placing my tiny digital recorder in my pocketbook, I struck out. I was determined to hit pay dirt—one way or another.

Smack—I ran directly into the Slarls. Because I was feeling frazzled and in such a hurry, I had forgotten to perform my usual reconnaissance. After slamming the door behind me, I turned to the right to make my way to the bridge. There they were drunkenly stumbling about. They must have lost the way to their own cabin.

Shielding my face with my purse, I attempted to rush past. Karl had different ideas. He grabbed my arm,

"Say schweetie, whash your hurry. Slu, I mean Mindy and I arsh looking for a little company, if you catsch my drift."

Slu—I mean Mindy—who had been licking his neck mumbled something while she continued to nuzzle him. Keeping my face averted, I yanked my arm away, mentioning that I was meeting someone and was now late. Karl, snickering at Mindy's sensual overtures, slurred,

"Perhaps we'll meet anusher time, shveetheart."

He showed no evidence of recognizing me. I waited a moment to ensure they didn't attempt to enter my cabin. They lurched down the hall, stumbling, giggling and snorting. They inserted their key card into every door latch they passed.

Ohhh boy-oh-boy, was that a close call!

On the bridge, Neal's striking face broke into a huge grin when he saw me. Since he was off duty, he no longer wore a uniform. Instead, he had on a sexy polo shirt and khakis, both of which flattered his muscular frame. A feast for eyes!

It was then that I realized the evening still had potential. With our arms entwined and a crystal goblet of sparkling wine in our other hand, we strolled along the deck and then back towards his cabin.

My glass flew from my hand! I had splatter wine over my new outfit!

With an unexpected thrust, he knocked me into the railing. I tried to grasp something, anything, in an attempt to stabilize myself. I was too much off balance.

Just then, another passenger appeared. The Good Samaritan grabbed my arm and pulled me back over the railing. In another moment, I would have been overboard, becoming flotsam and fish food.

Had the boat pitched?

Shaken, I thanked him. He was a chubby, older guy with graying and receding hair, but he looked beautiful to me. He responded to my stammered words of gratitude,

"And they say, smoking is hazardous to your health. Ha! Smoking just may have saved your life. I came out to light one up, just in the nick of time for you."

I turned and stared hard at Neal, who looked shaken himself. Something flickered in the back of his eyes as he rushed over. He wrapped his arms around me, holding me like he was afraid to let go. All memories of the mishap were erased as I stood there basking in the warmth of his strong arms.

But my radar continued to register ever enlarging blips.

Chapter 19

The sun was making its first morning appearance at the edge of the horizon when I made my way back to my room. I opened the door, anticipating diving into bed and catching a little sleep.

But, instead, I stood there *Stunned!*

"Ole," he said winking, perhaps in reference to our recent adventures in New Mexico, not that speaking Spanish had been a factor. Stretched out on my bed was none other than Saul! I lingered for a moment in the doorway while I gaped.

Saul's appearance was much different than during our last encounter. He was almost unrecognizable. I had grown accustomed to erratic behavior by my recent acquaintances. But never being prepared for whatever would happen next was often a little unnerving.

Recovering from my shock, I managed to ask, "What in heaven's name are you doing here? I thought you were creating an elaborate petroglyph exhibit at the Chicago Field Museum."

I was pretty certain that I wasn't going to care for the answer.

Saul responded,

"I finished the exhibit, so when Arturo called and shared his suspicion that you were following Karl, I decided to provide a little backup. Both Karl and his *bride* have a history of violence when subjected to pressure or when under the influence. Also, it might be easier to track their activities in Austria if there are two of us. In fact, there might soon be three. Arturo will join us once he gets out this month's issue of his magazine."

"How, where, and when did you get on board? Where will you stay? This cabin isn't big enough for both of us. It's barely large enough for one," I commented, suspecting that perhaps the continent wasn't large enough for the two of us at that moment.

"Oh, don't you worry. The cruise director and I are old friends. These philatelist cruises are never fully booked, as you might imagine. She managed to secure for me a cabin right next to yours. In fact they're adjoined. Arturo will stay with me. We figure it's safer for all of us to be in close proximity. Where have *you* been? I've been waiting for you for hours," he prodded,

Choosing not to answer, I just stared at him.

Breaking the silence, Saul queried,

"How do you like my new look, now that I've shaved my beard, cut my hair, and wear contacts? Makes me a little less easy to identify, don't you think? As for Arturo... I'm not certain how he intends to conceal his presence."

Saul not only looked different, he looked attractive! He no longer had the appearance of a freshly regurgitated hairball.

I reminded him,

"Well, despite your changed appearance, you're going to have to ditch your signature red scarf. There is no way Karl is *not* going to remember our Southwestern encounters if you keep that thing around your neck. That's the one he tried to strangle you with, remember? If I were you, I would burn it. That scarf must have bad karma."

Saul clutched his scarf protectively,

"Hey, I've got some good news for you. Remember the dealer who, four years ago, had a $2 million collection of rare 19th century stamps swiped from his rental car in Florida."

"Yes, I do..."

Saul continued,

"This past weekend, this guy learned that the FBI had arrested two men trying to sell part of the collection to a New York gallery. No one knows for sure how much of the collection they've recovered, or when the stamps might be returned. It was always suspected that the collection, which includes New York State 5-cent stamps issued in 1845 and Confederate State rarities valued at $400,000, would turn up when the thief tried to cash in.

"Stamps are like fingerprints. No two were alike, making them almost impossible to sell without discovery. FBI agents arrested two of the thieves after they sold some stamps to a New York gallery owner for $50,000. Authorities were tipped off about a month ago when these bozos tried to sell an additional $100,000 worth of stamps to another gallery owner. This one recognized the stamps as part of the stolen collection."

I asked,

"And this is good news for me... why?"

Ignoring my question, Saul continued,

"When the gallery owner told authorities about the collection offered to him, a special squad of FBI agents who investigate cases of stolen art, antiquities and other artifacts of high value acquired the case."

Grimacing, I commented,

"FBI agents seem to be crawling out of the walls of late, and their interests aren't confined to art theft. They recently arrested our aged, folksy pharmacist, Ozzi, on charges of Medicare fraud."

Now Ozzi had been known to bend the rules a little, but this was one of the qualities that were so endearing. If you needed a couple of pills advanced on your prescription refill because you, umm, took too many at one time by, umm, accident, Ozzie was there for you. But Ozzie had taken things one step further, I had learned. He was applying for reimbursements for prescriptions he hadn't filled.

But, I digress,

"Saul, the stamp caper you're describing sounds like one featured on the television show *Million Dollar Mysteries*."

Saul continued,

"This incident made headlines in the normally sedate world of stamp collecting because a former director of the American Philatelic Foundation considered it to be a major story. The victim was one of the largest and most reputable dealers of classic stamps.

"The victim of this particular crime was the leading stamp theft since 1998, when a New Mexican lawyer had a million-dollar collection of stamps and envelopes from 1869 snatched on a New York street. That collection—insured by the same company that insured the recently stolen collection—was recovered two years later!"

As an agent of Interpol, Saul persisted in flaunting his expertise,

"If the insurance company had already compensated the stamp proprietor for the total value of the collection, the insurer would take possession of the recovered stamps. To regain ownership of the collection, the dealer would then have to negotiate with the insurance company.

"This particular individual refused to discuss any settlement with the insurance company. He wanted his stamps back, and that was all there was to it.   An international dealer, he was an expert in stamps and postal history, especially in the classic U.S. classification.

"That category includes stamps printed before 1870. He maintained a detailed list of the stolen stamps on the Internet, having photographed and documented nearly all of them for their authenticity. They were rare. They were in demand. They were unique. He wanted them back."

I ventured,

"I can't say that I blame him. Wish to heck the Lünersee stamp collection had been so painstakingly documented."

Saul responded,

"I'm sure that it was, but the documentation was either stolen or destroyed by the Nazis. All serious collectors document their collections."

Chapter 20

When Saul returned to his cabin, I seized the opportunity to take a quick shower and snatch a nap. There were still several hours before dinner would be served when he returned, looking a little fresher.

We could not run the risk of being recognized on deck by you-know-who and you-know-who or the *You-know-whosies*. So we used the time to just relax and become reacquainted.

Saul then began to entertain me with stories of his Mid-East adventures from the days he conducted global rock-art research for his doctoral dissertation. Saul, the Chicago Field Museum petroglyph expert, jumped into the stories as if it had been yesterday when he was last there:

"While traveling from one place to another, we passed through a valley with a mound in it by name of Kadesh. Kadesh happened to be the site of a major battle between the Egyptians and the Hittites that took place around 1250 B.C.

"According to the Egyptians, they had won. They glorified the event by writing a description of the battle on the wall of one of their temples in Egypt. This was a practice just a little less primitive than writing on the wall of a cave."

The story had biblical overtones. I meant to ask if they used pictograms or petroglyphs to communicate, or did they have a written language at that time. But interrupting Saul is not an easy task...

"We also passed through Damascus. In the center of Damascus is a huge mosque. Built as a temple by the Romans, the structure was later converted into a Christian church. It was then made into a Moslem mosque, which it remains today. Within the mosque is a shrine said to contain the head of John the Baptist."

Other places claim to have his head too – two heads are better than one, yuk, yuk.

Saul continued his tale,

"In a street running alongside the mosque, you can see fragments of the Roman temple included in the foundation of the mosque. The mosque has a large courtyard surrounded by a wall which was also covered in mosaic. It was a very beautiful and impressive sight! I had seen Al Hombre in Spain, so was familiar with the beauty of mosaic tile patterns. In the souk (marketplace) of Damascus is a main street which the Bible refers to as a *straight*.

Street with an Appalachian accent?

"The area is covered with a metal roof full of bullet holes from the 1920s. That was when a French airplane fired on it in an attempt to put down an uprising. The souk itself is a large dark labyrinth where one can easily become lost, or can easily lose pursuers, as the case may be. It was here that I purchased my cylinder seal. Ahh, you look quizzical. You, perhaps, are wondering what a cylinder seal is? No?

"Well, let me tell you anyway. As its name indicates, it's a cylinder. Yes! It's carved from and engraved in stone. The surface is patterned with figures that tell a story when rolled on wet clay. These seals are characteristic artifacts of ancient Mesopotamian civilizations and are considered to be some of their finest artistic achievements. Another and perhaps more sophisticated form of rock art, to be sure."

"Perhaps we can consider it an automated form of rock art," I ventured.

Saul paused to chortle and then continued,

"Seals... not that kind, Canadians, put away your clubs... first appeared during the Protoliterate Period (c. 3400–2900 BC). The seal designs evolved from geometric, magical, or animal patterns to a variety of motifs that incorporated the owner's name. Sometimes the elements were arranged in symmetrical, decorative patterns that represented an action, very much in keeping with the rock art so typical in our southwest."

My question about its similarity to the rock art of the southwest had been answered.

"As time went on, besides recording an event, the seals were used to mark personal property and to make documents legally binding. Surrounding civilizations soon adopted their use. They were used for signatures.

"When returning to my hotel, I passed a butcher shop with all sorts of unsavory animal parts hanging outside. Just as I was about to enter the hotel, five men with rifles poured out of a white van which had just roared down the street. They burst into the building next door. I didn't hang around to see what might happen next."

Stretching and yawning, I said,

"Ahh, look at the time. We can go up to dinner now, and you can test your new look on Karl. Maybe we can continue your stories later."

My proposal sounded good to me.

Chapter 21

The meal was uneventful. We saw neither the Slarls nor my handsome navigator friend, Neal. Saul's new appearance went untested.

At least I didn't have to worry about Neal, the Navigator, seeing me with another man. Especially, after the strange evening, but most delightful night we spent together. I assumed the Slarls were still sleeping things off as well.

So, Saul and I continued our conversation. At my request, Saul picked up where he had left off with his description of his Middle Eastern adventures,

"Okay. To continue with Syria... Have you heard of Palmyra? No? Well, don't feel bad. Not too many people have. In antiquity, Palmyra was an important city in central Syria located in an oasis about 215 km northeast of Damascus and 180 km southwest of the Euphrates.

"How it evolved from being the *Town that Repels* to becoming the *Bride of the Desert* is something of a puzzle. But, everything is relative. The name Palmyra is thought to reference the palm trees growing there."

It was also the home of a woman who challenged Roman rule—possibly the first woman liber. I don't remember too much about that story.

Saul continued,

"The site, in addition to the ruins of the town, had a huge Temple complex devoted to the god Baal, who is considered to be one of the seven princes of Hell. Baal was ranked as the first and principal king in Hell, ruling over the East. The Old Testament gives frequent mention to him."

So, I thought, *they worshipped the devil. How interesting. I know just the hotel in Switzerland where they could enjoy some nice satanic artwork.*

To explain—on my previous adventures, I had, for lack of other lodging, spent the night in a Swiss hotel where every wall was adorned with pictures of the devil. They were sketches, not photos, the staff assured me. And, to top it off, there was a mysterious chateau high on a hill above the town. I could find not one person who would discuss anything about it.

Saul continued, unaware of my wondering thoughts,

"A bit further away, in a valley, there is a necropolis with unique tombs unlike anywhere else. The most impressive of the several styles are the tower tombs which are approximately four stories high. Inside the tombs are slots at all levels containing bodies. The bodies have since been moved to museums."

Saul paused to take a sip of wine. Having nothing better to do, I encouraged him to continue. And so he did,

"The museum in Damascus displays wonderful items, including Roman clothing taken from the tombs."

Oooh, trend setting! I made a mental face, since viewing clothing from tombs sounded grotesque.

"But the museum is not well maintained. Lighting is very poor and everything is coated with a layer of dust. The guard inside one of the museum corridors had his little stove on which to prepare tea."

I perked up at hearing the word *tea*, one of my favorite beverages and a means of survival at work. It is a huge help in fending off the mid-day drowsies.

Chapter 22

Saul continued,

"Tea and other beverages are an important part of Arabic culture. Tea breaks are a big deal in Syria. Tea is used for many purposes. During brisk negotiations in the souk, small glasses of extremely sweet tea will appear.

"Black tea is the most common, usually bearing the Lipton brand name. Another delicious tea, called *zouhourat*, is made from hibiscus flowers. This tea has a light yellow color and a delicate, flowery flavor.

"Sometimes used for stomach upset, tea also has a calming effect. Whether the effects are physical or psychological is debatable – much like our *drowsy-time* tea.

"Mint tea, the other tea found throughout the Arab world is brewed green tea served with mint leaves jammed in the glass with a liberal sprinkling of sugar. It is quite delicious."

Experiencing an enormous and sudden craving for tea, I signaled a waiter and ordered a pot of mint tea for two. A little sweet tea would set the ambiance for the remainder of the conversation.

Saul was enjoying himself. It was nice just to relax in the presence of familiar company. I had to admit to myself, I had been lonely.

Despite being a tad wordy, Saul's historical accounts were fascinating. He painted a visual picture of a part of the world I had never visited and where travel has become even more difficult for a westerner. Fortunately, the Nazis hid no treasures in the Middle East, at least to my knowledge.

After the tea arrived and we supped for a while, Saul continued his reminiscing,

"We passed a group of trailer trucks parked along the highway. All the drivers huddled by their stoves drinking tea. It was a scene reminiscent of ancient times, only with trucks instead of camels.

"Later, I visited the ruins of the city Dura Europus, which is as far east as the Romans ventured. In among the ruins we found a well-preserved painted wall from a synagogue (now in a museum). There was an early Christian church there too.

"Nothing is restored. The guard makes his rounds on a motorcycle, accompanied by just a shotgun and a tiny stove on which to make his tea."

I poured us each another cup. Saul took a sip and then continued,

"In the desert a short distance away are the ruins of the city of Resafa. Positioned on the caravan routes, it managed to flourish enough to later become a city."

Hmm, a regular metropolis!

"Because the community experienced constant conflicts between the Romans and Persians, the walls of the city were fortified with gypsum. It sparkled like a gem in the sunlight. The city looked like a mirage, like a magic kingdom rising abruptly from the desert plains."

Good thing the Nazis hadn't seen that city, I mused.

"Aside from its appearance, the city's most impressive feature was the system of underground cisterns that caught and stored the winter and spring rains.

"As is typical, nothing in Resafa is restored or modernized. There are no McDonalds or Kentucky Fried Chickens. If it is food you want, you have to bring it in yourself."

Yikes, how primitive! That settles it. I'm never traveling to such "barbarous" countries myself.

Saul continued,

"In northern Syria there is an area with many ruins of towns and other features. The church complex named for St. Simeon is very impressive. It sits high on a ridge above the plains of southern Turkey—great view.

"Much of the architecture has survived in good condition and is very interesting. St. Simeon lived on top of a tall stone column. Pilgrims would come to visit, bringing him food and water."

I interrupted, aloud this time,

"Do you think if we sat on the column, someone would bring us food?"

Fascinating though the information was, after a period, I began to feel like I was sitting in a lecture hall. I began to squirm.

Ignoring my fidgeting, Saul continued,

"Today, all that remains of the column is a short nub. Since few other tourists visit here so the site remains pristine. Another remote site here is Ain Dara—a mound with a Hittite temple on top.

These sites were not as remote as my day dreaming was becoming. I was envisioning a romp through the park, shopping online... What had been an enticing narration was turning into monotonous droning to my exhausted ears.

Nevertheless, the oral assault continued,

"The Hittites were a Bronze Age Indo-European speaking people who established a kingdom in what is now northern Syria. The Hittite temple entrance has a stone slab with carvings of a person's feet. This is where the god entered. It's a very unusual and mysterious ruin."

Feeling that a periodic response was necessary for the sake of etiquette, I ventured,

"If your feet fit the foot carvings, did you receive a blessing?"

I quickly moved on,

"What a shame Syria is such an awful mess."

Saul mused, more to himself than to me,

"At that time, I felt safe walking alone in Damascus and Hama. Hama, now there's a place. Hama is famous for its 15th century giant water wheels, many of which still work."

Oh, Yeah! There we go—water wheels—my passion— not.

"Then there is Ugarit, an ancient port city on the eastern Mediterranean, another fascinating primordial city. Tablets found at Ugarit were written in the last period of its life (around 1300 - 1200 BCE). I was fortunate enough to see the original tablet showing our modern alphabet."

That style of writing was known as alphabetic cuneiform. This is a unique blending of an alphabetic script (like Hebrew) and cuneiform, like Akkadian, an extinct Semitic language.

Saul continued,

"There is a strong possibility that the alphabetic cuneiform came into being as cuneiform was passing from the scene and alphabetic scripts were making their rise.

"I felt privileged to witness the transition from communication through crude sketching and engraving on rocks to a primitive written language."

"Fascinating," I said, stifling a yawn.

"In one place I was able to walk through a building complex 4000 years old. It was there that I bought a unique and rare azure cylinder seal. You wouldn't believe the detail contained on such a small piece of stone."

I interrupted,

"Oh, yes I would. Would you compare the seal to an ancient stamp?"

His response,

"Mm... it's probably more the equivalent of a signature or an indication of the 'return address.'"

All this chatter about the Middle East stimulated a flashback to my encounter with the handsome Turk in Morocco. I wondered what devious acts Muhammad was engaged in right now.

Then I recollected the mysterious character in the Joliet courthouse. Those haunting blue eyes had looked *very* familiar. I decided to search my clothing and pocket book for transmitters.

When Saul paused, I whined,

"Well, at least you were there, even if it's not the same now as it was then. I envy you all those experiences."

For neither rhyme nor reason, other than being victimized by a wandering mind, I began fretting the likelihood of having been bugged. I pondered whether the court house stranger could have been the striking looking Turk, Muhammad, whom I had crossed paths with in Algiers.

Nah!

I suspected he had planted a tracking and listening device on my handbag at that time. The result was that Karl and slut-woman appeared at each of our destinations either ahead of or simultaneously with us.

The timing was very suspicious, indeed. And had I not encountered in the courtroom during jury duty a mysterious person? A person whose face, in part, was obscured with a scarf? A person with piercing blue eyes that were so reminiscent of Muhammad's?

Saul's lecture came to an abrupt halt. Clearly irritated, he glared at me,

"Do you always jiggle your knee when someone else is speaking?"

He paused, then said,

"Oh, man, now I understand where you're coming from. I'm losing my voice from talking so much."

On that note, Saul gave up and got up. Giving me a peck on the check, he bade me a good night. I was left at the table with my own thoughts, which, of course, wandered back to the topic of stamps and treasures.

Having finished the last dregs of tea, I, too, left the dining area and returned to my cabin. Because it was fairly late, there were not many people moving about in my section of the ship.

The artificial lighting generated eerie shadows.

Casting suspicious glances over my shoulder, I quickened my pace when I thought I heard someone behind me. The cadence of another set of footsteps seemed to keep pace with mine. I became nervous. Every corner developed the potential to conceal a malfeasance.

At last, arriving back at the room unscathed, I peeked in my closet to check for lurkers. I then gave the lock one final turn.

After bidding Saul goodnight through the adjoining door, I sat down and fired up the old laptop. Sometimes the internet seems more of a curse than a blessing, enslaving most who come in contact with it.

Chapter 23

It took a mere five minutes in my cabin to realize that I was not sleepy enough to turn in. Since it was a philately cruise, I decided to wonder about. Maybe I could find a few good displays or watch an exciting stamp auction unfold.

Instead of exercising either of those options, I wandered into one of the philately lectures. This one was entitled Tales of Arabian stamps. I was amazed to see guards armed with scimitars lining the walls. I couldn't decide if they were body guards or were there to keep the strained-looking lecturer from escaping.

I regretted that Saul was not there with me since he had such a fascination with the Middle East. I took a seat in the back.

The evolution of stamps in the Middle East promised to be captivating. Although a little remote from the subject of the Lünersee stamps, how fascinating it would be to learn about stamp intrigues from that area. Stories akin to *Ali Baba and the Forty stamps* or the *Arabian Philatelists*.

Another consideration was that a Middle Eastern stamp could have been a part of the Lünersee collection. It soon became evident that, despite the ancient civilizations and the 8000 year history of the region, Middle Eastern stamps are relatively recent.

In the 1840's, the area that constitutes present day Turkey issued the Ottoman Empire's very first stamp. However, the Middle Eastern country stamps collected today didn't originate until well into the 20th Century.

Inspired by Britain's successful introduction in 1840 of the universal penny stamp, Middle Eastern nations aspired to similar postal bureaucracies. Emirates and kings wasted no time trying to revolutionize their postal systems. They adopted the adhesive style stamp and eliminated private courier services.

During the late 1800s, Emirates contracted with private international printers to craft special Middle East stamp series to sell to international collectors. Iraq, granted its own private postal service by the League of Nations just after World War I, produced its first series of stamps in 1923.

These stamps featured King Faisal I. Iraq ran another series of stamps in 1927 and 1931, again honoring King Faisal I—at *the directive of King Faisal I, no doubt.*

When Iraq declared its independence in 1932, the government issued new stamps and currency, both of which again, surprise, *honored King Faisal I.*

In 1934, when a new ruler, King Ghazi, gained power in Iraq, he was content to share the *postal stage* with his predecessor on the next run of stamps. Following Ghazi's unexpected death in 1941, the government scrambled to issue stamps of nature scenes.

When Saddam Hussein gained power in the late 1970s, almost every Iraqi stamp minted during the 1980s featured his face or some allusion to his greatness.

Following the successful American toppling of Saddam's regime in 2002, the Iraqi government stopped producing Saddam Era stamps and relied on Coalition transition stamps.

This description of the emergence of stamp usage in the Middle East reaffirmed the conviction that one could track the history of a nation through its postal stamps.

According to the lecturer, collecting Middle East stamps becomes ever more enticing. This is especially true when the other option is an excursion to those parts. The increased cost of travel coupled with rising political tensions among Western and Middle Eastern countries, inhibits many from journeying to the Middle East.

"Collecting stamps or memorabilia from these countries is one of the few ways many may have to experience the historical and cultural wonders of those regions."

The professor looked wistful as he uttered those last words.

As I was the only non-Middle Easterner in the room, I felt he was directing those comments to me.

Wonder if he needs help escaping? I mused, looking again at the armed-to-the–teeth guards lining the room.

Chapter 24

The next morning found me slumped over my computer. I awakened with a stale taste in my mouth, but to the fragrance of fresh-brewed coffee. That scent made the morning's arrival almost tolerable. My first emotion was one of concern over the time spent the previous night researching stamps from the Middle East. My focus should be on Austria, where the Lünersee stamps are reputed to be hidden.

Prying open first one eye, and then the other, I thought with a start that I was seeing a distorted double. Was that Arturo standing next to Saul? Saul who had resurfaced in my life just the previous day? I blinked once, then again. He was still there. They were both still there.

Saul came over, placed his hand on my shoulder, handed me a cup of coffee, and advised me to take a quick shower. They had ordered breakfast for the three of us, so bade me to hurry before it grew cold.

Too tired and confused to protest, and because breakfast provided a powerful incentive, I showered in record time. After throwing on some fresh clothes, I stumbled into their room.

Saul and I had chatted extensively yesterday. Arturo and I didn't have much catching up to do since we were in daily contact regarding assignments, deadlines, and so forth. I *was* curious to know how he managed to appear on board since we were pretty far from shore. Although an accomplished scuba diver, I doubted that he had swum the distance.

Having adjoining rooms was great. I didn't have to worry as much about running into Karl and S-woman when looking for Arturo and Saul.

We sat around slugging down coffee. Saul described how, during the course of his relationships at the Chicago Field Museum with his colleagues, he stumbled across useful material. It was information that might help protect us from additional break-ins. Not including the unpleasant circumstance in the hall, I had at least two other scary encounters since beginning the Lünersee stamp quest. And those were break-ins.

We both stared at Saul, waiting for him to continue. When he didn't, I gave him an irritable nudge. Through a mouthful of eggs, Saul explained that while working in close proximity and associating with other museum researchers, he had come across information that, though not related to stamps and treasures, we might find useful.

He went on to describe his "exciting" news,

"Researchers have discovered a new antibacterial under the skin of frogs that emit a particularly foul odor. Tests have proven this substance to be effective against a broad spectrum of bacteria that have become resistant to the most commonly used antibiotics: i.e., amoxicillin, erythromycin, etc.

"The theory is that since frogs often live in waters saturated with bacteria, their bodies secrete peptides under the skin. These peptides having antibacterial properties protect them from infection and bacterial-related diseases. An evolutionary quality—survival of the fittest, if you will."

"Fascinating," I said. "How is this information relevant to us?"

"Well, for one thing," Saul said, "this subject would make a great article for Arturo's magazine. He could commission you to write the article, and in the course of interviewing and researching, you could be carrying around a small sample. You could say that you need to have a lab in Europe corroborate the results."

I interrupted,

"Who would care enough about my knocking around the continent that I would need to provide a sample of stinky frog gunk as an excuse? And how will this product protect me from break-ins?"

Saul replied,

"Good question. We'll think of something. Mostly, this provides you with a cover story. If anyone, one of the Slarls, for instance, is suspicious of your activities, just tell them that you're conducting research. You are interviewing European scientists familiar with the substance in preparation for the writing of an article. And besides, remember, that the little bugger stinks. And, so does the test sample. Just offering a whiff during a break in would be enough of a distraction to enable escape or a defense opportunity."

I said,

"Well, what about you two? What sort of cover will you have? And I still don't see why I should need an excuse for the Slarls."

Arturo, who had been silent until now, reminded me that he and Arturo were Interpol agents. They have the ability to fade in and out of scenarios at any time an investigation dictated. They have resources and contacts that most do not.

With that aide-memoire, I felt a more secure in their company. But, until I authenticated their credentials by putting in a call to Interpol, I was reluctant to have them around if and when I recovered the stamps.

I had mixed feelings about their presence since I didn't want Interpol laying claim to the stamps. I was certain that they would preempt my plans to return the stamps to the original owner's heirs. Interpol would end up turning them over to some government or other. I wanted to restore the stamps to the heirs of those who perished at Dachau.

Perhaps I would request that my Washington contact get in touch with the international organization to authenticate Karl and Saul's identities. I should have done that many months ago.

If they checked out, I would have them swear that they wouldn't lay claim to the stamps. They would have to promise to help me restore them to their owners. Of course that may cause a moral dilemma for them. Their allegiance to Interpol would require turning in the stamps to close the cold case.

****

Eww! Saul hadn't explained in adequate terms how smelly the antibacterial producing tiny frogs were. He happened to have such a little creature in a container in his room. He felt that a live specimen would make his information more convincing to Arturo and me.

Cute little bugger at first glance, but when I caught a whiff of Fred-the-frog's scent, I threw open the port window. Breathing in the fresh river air, I concluded that this little amphibian represented one of the nastiest smelling creatures on Earth. The fact that it had the ability to produce the greatest known variety of anti-bacterial peptide substances didn't negate the fact that it stank.

These tiny critters have the potential for becoming new weapons in the battle against antibiotic-resistant infections, but they smell like rotten fish. In fact, next to them, in my esteemed opinion, skunks emit an odor comparable to a Parisian perfume.

Perfume... an idea was forming. Perhaps Mrs. *Slarl* would like to try a dab of *exotic* perfume behind her ears or in her over-exposed cleavage.

I'm not vindictive by nature, but I still hadn't recovered from the Slarls planting a bugging device on me, then attempting to convince me that they had met their demise. First, Karl had pretended to be poisoned when I went to visit him, and then his *lovely* wife feigned her own death by faking a fatal fall into a kiva in New Mexico.

At that time, we were seeking to decipher the clue to either the Lünersee stamps' identity or location. The clue had been left in my bag while I was on my way to Sweden. It was a series of sketches similar to the art found in the caves and cliffs of that area in New Mexico.

And, if that weren't enough, slut-woman had read and answered emails that I had sent to Karl—a definite no-no in my book. Oh, had I already mentioned that—several times in fact? And then there was the matter of an assassin.

Chapter 25

It appears that Chinese scientists have identified approximately nine species of stinky frogs that secrete more than 700 peptide substances with antibacterial powers. This represents an approximate one-third of all antibacterial peptides worldwide. Some of the peptides have a dual action, killing bacteria directly while activating the immune system to assist in the battle.

Saul continued,

"And since we're on the very special topic of bacteria, have you heard about the New Brunswick researcher's claims that bacteria from the Bay of Fundy are showing promise as potential cancer-fighting agents?

"They discovered this property while searching for marine bacteria that could help protect young fish in the salmon farming industry. Some of the bacterial extracts that were good for salmon have the potential of protecting humans from cancer and infectious bacteria.

"You know, marine bacteria are difficult to grow, so, by using the same strain, a researcher explored other possible uses for marine bacteria. He found that some of those bacteria produce chemicals that test positive for both antibiotic and anti-cancer effects. Scientists are now in the process of ramping up production so that they have more of the compound to conduct experiments to further analyze the properties.

"The neat thing about bacteria is that they can have quite complex biochemistries. Their systems allow them to synthesize some very complicated molecules that we can't, or that we can only synthesize with the greatest of difficulty and at great expense.

"Bacteria could be a very renewable, sustainable, better manufacturing system for the production of antibiotics, better than anything we've seen—ever! So," Saul said with great excitement, "What do you think?"

Arturo and I just stared at each other and then at Saul.

As if about to display great wisdom and insight, I said, "Um..."

I then snapped,

"To quote an old saying, what does this have to do with the price of tea in China? Or, taking it a bit further, how does this have anything to do with the Lünersee stamps?"

Saul looked at me,

"Woman, have you no imagination? This little frog can protect us. Once my contact at the University of Chicago Medical School determines which bacteria may be susceptible to the secretions of our new anti-bacterial friends, the stinky frogs, then we can use these same bacteria to infect and disable any pursuers, while using the new froggy-produced antibiotics to become impervious to infection ourselves."

"What," I squeaked, "Is this ethical? You could start a pandemic that way."

Things were becoming a bit complicated. Arturo suppressed a chuckle. Saul looked as though he were ready to throttle me.

He exclaimed,

"Darlin, we are dealing with criminals and potential murderers. And you're worried if what we are doing is ethical?"

I said,

"Well, we would need a lot more information and what about clinical trials? How do we know these antibacterial substances work the way they're supposed to without killing us in the process—or making us stink forever?"

No one had asked me to, but I continued anyway,

"I think using a fungus or poison mushrooms are more prudent approaches. With a little research, we can either grow or find them ourselves. That way there would be little chance of leaving a traceable trail. A few spores here, a few spores there... And, besides, you're Interpol agents. You have to uphold the law! I've never taken that oath."

They just looked at each other. Then at last, Arturo broke the silence.

"You may be right," he said in his slow measured and accented tones, "but maybe we should have some of dis antibacterial compound as a preventative measure. Maybe we're not de only ones thinking in dese terms. Didn't Karl used to be a microbiologist or some kind of biotech engineer? He may have access to some virulent cultures and be planning to infect at least you."

Me?

Arturo continued,

"When Saul and I conducted a background check, we noticed dat his employment was associated wit some mysterious illnesses in coworkers. Dese coworkers were up for the same promotion as he. In one instance, de person died."

He stared in a deliberate manner at me before continuing.

"Wouldn't it be good to have some effective antibiotic wid us at all times, just in case? Dis Karl is a little more ruthless dan you are admitting, yes?"

Damn that Karl! I can just see it now. Someone pulls out a gun on us, and we pull out this itty-bitty frog.

I was still more interested in our little amphibious traveling companion for his putrid smell. I had great plans for the use of its *fragrance*. But I did agree in theory that it wouldn't hurt to have an effective antibiotic readily accessible, just in case.

Go, harvest the little guy's antibiotics, but I have other plans for little froggy's secretions.

I left for my own room, but first encouraged Saul,

"Get your little frog beastie busy producing, excreting, secreting his own very special essence."

I chortled to myself, *Essence de Froggy... Essence de Grenouille.*

Chapter 26

I spent most of my day researching perfume bottles and perfume solutions, determined to conjure up a little *scented* fun. Having had the opportunity to observe slut-woman first hand, I had determined that she was egotistical enough to think that a personalized perfume would enhance her efforts to express her individuality.

And she was the type of woman who would respond favorably to receiving a gift from a *secret admirer,* or any admirer for that matter.

While perusing the ship's shops, I stumbled across a perfume specialty store called *Scentseekers.* The employees were trained to assist cruise customers craft their own perfumes using a three-step process.

The *Seeker* could choose from several options. For example, I could either describe the effect I wanted to create, or I could select specific scents. Since sharing the *effect I* was shooting for would not be prudent, I selected the *specific* option.

Scanning through the selections—Masculine, Mixed, Flowers, Miscellaneous, Exotic—I determined that *Exotic* might be the appropriate terminology. The definition for the word *exotic* includes unusual, outlandish, mysterious, and bizarre.

Since slut-woman was an egotist, I concluded that her mind would focus on the *mysterious* description. From the list of selections under *mysterious*, I selected *Acid Rain.* That name sounded ominous and was ambiguous enough to suit my purposes.

I was then presented with the option of one of two *recipes.* The first recipe was male oriented. It included *Hugo Boss* and almond. Recipe Number Two sounded a little more feminine. It included Apple Blossom, Gardenia, and Lilac scents.

Why was I being so fussy? My *secret* ingredient would, no doubt, overpower all delicate scents. I decided it was all about the creative process.

The final steps involved naming the newly minted scent and choosing a bottle for it. The bottle color was no problem. S-woman seemed to have a strong preference for hot pink, so pink it was.

But, to come up with a tantalizing name: Hmmm, how about *Essence of You...* or *Essence of P.U.*? Not bad. Maybe not subtle, but quite appropriate.

Placing my order, I went the more conservative route and instructed the employees to name the fragrance *Essence of.* I also advised them that there was no need to deliver. I would be picking up,

"Just buzz me on my cell."

An oversized hat, sunglasses, and a moo-moo with a pillow under it strapped to my waist completed my disguise. I then sauntered up to the deck and settled into a chair, awaiting the appearance of the honeymooners.

After several hours, suffering from too much sun and extreme thirst, I abandoned my project. I assumed that the Slarls were recovering from another heavy night of drinking.

I had not yet heard from the specialty perfume boutique. I ambled over to the shopping district to check on the progress of my own special concoction. It was ready. I paid with cash, of course.

The final product, made to my specifications, was quite enchanting looking. And it smelled so lovely, for now... *heh. heh.* Maybe I could pour a little out, reserving an unadulterated portion for myself before adding my *secret* ingredient to the delicate little bottle.

Now, to get froggy to produce some essence for me. I didn't want to hurt the little guy, nor did I want to traumatize him. His antibiotic producing skills could be in big demand later in the trip.

If I just extracted a little of the water he swims in and add it to the vial, it would create the desired effect.

I knew that Mindy would, in gluttonous haste, dump most of the noxious mix on her person before first stopping to sample the scent.

I used just the tiniest amount of *Essence le Froggy*, and, what had been an incredibly sweet smelling *Acid Rain* now stank like an authentic and toxic acid rain.

Still in my disguise, I sought out a member of the kitchen staff, one whom I did not expect to encounter on a frequent basis.

I flashed a twenty in front of him and asked for a little, itty-bitty favor. He was more than happy to deliver the vial accompanied by the card identifying the gifter as *Your Secret Admirer.*

I had instructed him to just place the exotic-looking package outside their cabin door. That way he wouldn't be subjected to interrogation from Karl, or the ear-piercing squeals and giggles from a delighted Mindy Slutkowski-*Slarl.*

I sat back, waiting for my concoction to work its magic. Since I suspected that there would be low water pressure for several days as slut-woman tried to wash away the disgusting potion, I decided to take an immediate shower myself. But, who knows, perhaps the Slarls would like my creation.

Chapter 27

It was time to become serious and for us to begin mapping strategies. Because of my research and the picture bearing coordinates I had received in the mail, we had several sites in addition to Lake Lünersee to explore.

I had also gathered additional information about the Amber Room. I was developing a real affinity for this treasure, as well as for the Lünersee stamps. I was intrigued, not by the obvious value, but by its exquisite beauty.

This treasure, when prioritizing, should rise to near the top of the list, becoming second only to the stamps. The newest description of the Amber Room that I had stumbled upon was more detailed and intriguing than any former one.

Previous information described the Amber Room as being ornate and constructed with hundreds of pieces that fit together like a puzzle. The latest account portrayed the unparalleled room as being comprised of a series of large wall panels. These were inlaid with several tons of masterfully carved high-quality amber, long wall mirrors, and four Florentine mosaics.

The amber covered not one, but three walls and was arranged in three tiers. The central (middle) tier consisted of eight large, symmetrical vertical panels. Four of them contained pictures made of semiprecious stones, like quartz, jasmine, jade and onyx, executed in the 1750s in Florence.

The technique used was the Florentine mosaic, a technique similar to that used by the artist Giuseppe Dzokki. The panels are said to depict the five senses: Sight, Taste, Sound, Touch, and Smell.

The distance between the large panels was occupied by mirrored pilasters. The room's bottom tier was covered in square amber panels.

When its 565 candles were lit, the Amber Room was said to *glow a fiery gold*. I was wondering what material was used in the construction of the fourth wall. Mirrors reflecting the brilliance of the other three walls would have been an excellent touch.

The room's original furnishings were no less spectacular than the room itself. A small amber table with elegantly turned legs rested in one corner.

The remainder of the room was adorned with inlaid wooden stands and seats of vintage Russian. An antique porcelain Chinese vase rested on another of the tables.

As if that weren't enough, one of the most valuable collections of amber objects created in the 17th and 18th centuries by German, Polish, and Russian masters was housed in the room's glass-covered display cases.

What an elegant exhibition this must have been. My interest intensified. This treasure was just too exquisite to lie in a state of decay, either underground or under water.

Chapter 28

Incredible! There was an *Amber Room* club*!* This organization was founded with the sole purpose of tracking down the dissembled room. To date, they had recorded the following,

> *The German official in charge of the amber shipment said the crates were in a castle that burned down in an air raid. But, documents found around February 4, 1945, revealed that the army reported that the 40 wagons from Konigsberg were undamaged in the attack. They were seen moving down to Auerswalde under conditions of the greatest secrecy.*
> *Club members then found documents stating that captured Soviet POWS, a hundred of them, were detailed to unload the crates from the train and store them in an underground facility in woods outside the town.*

There are records of an S.S. detachment being sent down to guard this operation. The report went further,

> *Deliveries: Researchers found details of secret Nazi shipments to Chemnitz which may have included the Amber Room.*

Chemnitz is less than ten miles from Auerswalde, one of our destinations. How very convenient for me. I should say, for us! That is also where divers discovered a $100,000 gold cauldron thought to have belonged to a high-ranking Nazi official.

An Auerswalde resident, now well into his 80s said about the Germans,

> The Germans had this kind of operation so late into the war suggests that something very valuable, indeed, was in those crates. This was the time that the transport system was descending into chaos.
> Deep in the Muna forest outside of town, there was a massive shelter built for munitions works employees. I went there as a boy. The shelter was massive, big enough

for trucks to turn around. It vanished off the maps after the war, but I and my friend Hans-Peter found a ventilation shaft leading down into an underground structure. We think it is the old shelter.

If the shipment from Koenigsberg that was guarded by the S.S. was unloaded here, then we owe it to history to open it up and look.

Oh, yeah!

If it were not the Amber Room secreted and stored there, it could be the diamonds and gold sought with so much eagerness by others. The books and maps Hans-Peter found amid the items of his father, the Luftwaffe signaler, support the existence of such a treasure. These artifacts document local reports of how German military convoys hid heavy sealed caskets in the mines on April 9, 1945.

****

There are other mines thought to house stolen treasure. During World War II, German troops invaded and looted the bank reserves of numerous countries across Europe. They took the gold back to Germany. They also stripped victims of the holocaust of all valuables, including fine jewelry.

They melted down the collected gold resources, casting them into bars imprinted with the mark of the German Central Bank, the Reichsbank. The Germans used many of these assets to pay for the war effort, but large unused portions remained in Nazi hands as the war ended.

In February of 1945 the President of the Reichsbank sent the majority of the gold reserves to the village of Merkers some 200 miles south of Berlin. There it was concealed in a deep underground potassium mine. The mine was also used to store many art treasures, some belonging to German museums, others looted from conquered nations.

In April of 1945, Merkers was captured by the U.S. Third Army commanded by Lieutenant General George Patton. French civilians working at the mine described to the American military what was hidden there. The hoard was soon in American hands.

It is estimated that the treasure consisted of 8,198 bars of gold bullion in the mine. In addition to gold coins, there were silver bars, and paper money. The total value *in 1945 dollars* was estimated to be over $520 million. This constituted the bulk of the Nazi loot, but not all of it.

Some of the gold and other valuables remained in Berlin. *Has the US tried hard enough to return its share of the loot to the countries from which it was stolen?*

Chapter 29

I sat on a deck chair and pondered.

Why hadn't I heard a reaction to my lovely gift of scent, Essence de Froggy, to slut-woman? I wasn't expecting a thank you note, but my creation warranted some audible reaction.

A terrible thought occurred.

Perhaps she had re-gifted the perfume. Oh well, there was no hard evidence that had happened. I was being impatient.

Just then a piercing shriek disrupted the tranquil environment. Fearing for my eardrums, I placed a pillow over my head. I could hear doors slamming and there was shouting—much shouting. I could only speculate and hope. My mouth spread into a slow, broad, anticipatory grin.

Feeling pretty good about myself, I decided it might be best, for the foreseeable future and for obvious reasons, to keep an even lower profile. I covered my knees with my bright pink mu-mu and forced myself to continue reading.

Then, again, this was a philatelic cruise. I should be attending more philatelic activities. Who knows what I might learn. As I stood, I noticed something near my chair.

Wait. Is that a stamp on the floor? Someone must have dropped it. How unusual! I wonder if it's worth anything.

I reached down to pick it up when one of a pair of highly polished shoes stepped on it.

Looking up, I recognized the Middle Eastern philatelic professor.

"Where are the guards?" I queried.

"The guards were not for me, Miss."

Just then, for no obvious reason, he turned on his heel and walked off.

I stared for a moment, then shrugged and continued to peel the stamp off the floor. In possession of my new treasure, I walked off in the opposite direction.

Chapter 30

Lake Toplitz, as previously noted, is a cold, deep, dark, one mile long lake settled between steep limestone cliffs in the Salzkammergut region in Austria. It is a beautiful, but remote area. At the depth of over 300 feet deep, its dark, deep recesses and isolated location induce the feeling that the lake is the perfect place to hide something. The Germans thought so.

When it happened, everyone in the village knew what had occurred and exactly where. They knew who had done it and why. And while they continued to tell the story over the years, an unsettling doubt arose, which grew as if from a half-heard whisper. Had it ever happened at all?

The story of how crates suspected of containing Nazi treasure came to be submerged in that lake is a fascinating one. It reads like something from a spy novel,

> One very early morning in 1945, deep in the Austrian Alps, there was a sharp rap on the door. It was the door of the only farm house around for many miles.
>
> A young 21 year old, pink-cheeked Austrian farm girl lived there with her family. When she answered the door, she was confronted by a small gathering of German officers with many large crates balanced on a series of trucks.
>
> "Come immediately," a soldier barked at her, "Hitch up the horse wagon. We need you. Schnell!"
>
> Afraid not to comply, the obedient, slight young woman did as instructed and pulled the family wagon up next to a military vehicle. Soldiers then loaded the heavy boxes onto the wagon.
>
> Curiosity gnawed at her. The only markings on the plain crates were numbers and some Cyrillic lettering, giving no hint as to the contents.
>
> They loaded the wagon. Then the officer told the girl to drive it to nearby Lake Toplitz. Once she was provided the destination, the need for the wagon became obvious to her: Only a horse-drawn wagon could traverse the rough terrain from the road to the lake.

She was finished after three trips. On the last trip, the young Austrian woman noticed that soldiers were dropping the crates into the lake. For many years afterwards, she pondered over what secrets those watery depths concealed.

****

Were the boxes seen by Ida Eisenbacher filled with some of the missing gold? Nobody knows for certain what was inside. Some believe they contained gold looted by German troops throughout Europe and carried back to Germany.

Others speculate that they contain documents showing where assets confiscated from Jewish victims were hidden in Swiss bank accounts. When divers did go down to investigate, they found not gold, but crates of counterfeit British pounds, secret documents, along with a printing press.

Curious treasure hunters have flocked to picturesque Lake Toplitz ever since. They are determined to unravel the mystery of what that group of diehard Nazis hid there in the final months of the Second World War.

Those boxes, sunken so many years ago, have inspired expeditions, as well as numerous books and movies. Several mysterious deaths are associated with the lake.

Anyone thinking *Odessa*, or scarier still, *DKDKD*? Either of these groups would kill to protect or abscond with a treasure of great value.

Chapter 31

More Lakes means more treasures. In April of 1945 when the Allies were closing in on the German capital, Nazi officials moved the remaining gold and currency of the Reichsbank to southern Bavaria. They planned to regroup there in the mountains.

The Nazis hid the estimated nine tons of gold in the form of gold bars, along with bags of foreign currency and coins, around Lake Walchensee. After the end of the war, U.S. soldiers found and accounted for $11 million of that final hoard. Over $3 million remains undiscovered. The theory that escaping Nazi officials smuggled some of the loot out of the country when they were fleeing the allies is a good one.

It is now more than 60 years since Nazi officers dropped the metal boxes into the depths of Lake Toplitz. Adventurers, once again, are organizing another attempt to recover the lost riches of the Third Reich.

A US team has received permission from the Austrian government to explore the log-glutted lake bottom. They hope to solve the 60-plus year-old mystery.

According to Norman Spott, an American treasure hunter,

"I really don't know if there is anything down there, but we want to resolve the mystery once and for all. We intend to first measure the lake."

He added,

"This is a beautiful area. You have heard of Loch Ness. For Austrians, this has been a bit like Loch Ness. Lots of people come here. And whether there is gold down there or not, the mystery has been very good for tourism.

"Any treasure found will be divided between the Americans and the Austrian state with the added stipulation, that, if we recover anything which has an identifiable owner, under Austrian law we must return it."

Mr. Spott, the American explorer, plans a detailed underwater survey of the 107 meter (350ft) deep lake.

I, Elyse, may be part of this historic event, having received an invitation from the team leader. My journalist credentials and the tiny bit of publicity generated by my connection with the Lünersee Stamp hunt have flung open a few doors in the treasure hunting arena.

This is a small consolation for also having a contract levied upon me. This was knowledge gleaned during an overheard cruise conversation.

Perhaps, the invitation to dive and the contract are one and the same. Explorations in this lake have proven deadly. In 1947 a US navy diver became entangled in Lake Toplitz's many submerged logs and drowned.

Other expeditions fared better. In 1959, a team financed by the German magazine *Stern,* had better luck, retrieving £72m in forged sterling currency hidden in boxes, and a printing press. The currency, it turned out, was part of the secret counterfeiting operation, Operation Bernhard.

Chapter 32

Adolf Hitler personally authorized Operation Bernhard. It was an attempt to weaken the British economy and in part pay for the war effort. At least, as a discovered *treasure*, sterling silver might have value. Other than as a collectible, the counterfeit currency would have no value.

The Nazis imported prisoners with special skills from all over Europe to make the counterfeit money. Adolph Burger, a former prisoner at Sachsenhausen concentration camp recounted his experiences in a book, which was turned into an Oscar-winning movie called *The Counterfeiters*, a very poignant movie. At age 92, Burger is the only remaining living worker from the *Devil's Factory*, as he referred to it.

The SS arrested Burger in 1942 in Slovakia. What was his crime? A printer, he helped Jews falsify documents to keep his Jewish clients, as well as others, out of the concentration camps. He and his wife ended up in a camp themselves as a result.

When they arrived at Auswitch, they were split up. The women went to one side; the men to the other. Burger soon learned that his wife was sent directly to the crematorium that very first day.

Auswitch was a living hell where the infamous Dr. Mengele experimented on the prisoners. Even though not a twin, Burger was on his list.

Burger received a Typhus vaccine which made him very ill. He only escaped the crematorium because he was hidden in the hay in the barracks by his friends. Five others who also had become ill were sent to the crematorium.

While in Auschwitz, the Nazis began looking for prisoners with printing experience. Almost immediately, Burger, who had been known only as prisoner 6440, a non-entity to be experimented upon, became *Mr. Burger*.

He was told,

"Mr. Burger, the Reich is entrusting you with a secret mission for the Fatherland."

The number had now become a person. According to Burger, only a select few knew about them.

Burger and three others with printing skills arrived from Auswitch to Sachsenhausen. There were two barracks behind two layers of barbed-wire fence and internal security.

The Nazis gave the counterfeiters special treatment, when compared to the other prisoners. They were allowed to shower once a week and they received adequate food and slept on actual beds with sheets and blankets. Those who would accept them received and wore the clothes confiscated from other prisoners who met their fate in the gas chambers.

When the *elite* prisoners were taken to the showers, the guards locked everyone else in the barracks. No one was supposed to see the special prisoners, counterfeiters, or be aware of what they were doing.

As additional incentive, the elite counterfeiting prisoners received a ping pong table and permission to create a carnival, where some of the prisoners displayed their talents for the amusement of the others.

One of Burgers friends drew a picture of Adolf at the camp. Burger kept the drawing as a reminder to the prisoners of what can happen when a population becomes vulnerable.

Their *luxuries* may seem simplistic, but not if you factor in that other prisoners of the Nazis were being experimented upon, starved and executed on a daily basis. In comparison, their meager privileges looked like extravagances.

Bernard Kruger, the important SS officer who ran the counterfeit-money operations, reported to Himmler. He explained to the prisoners their duties, adding the footnote that anyone trying to sabotage the mission would meet with a swift and fatal punishment.

A cruel individual, Kruger was responsible for many deaths—deaths that were never avenged.

Burger regarded his relationship with Kruger as one between the executioner and the victim. Despite being better fed, allowed to grow out hair, and having access to cigarettes on occasions, many SS officers hated and wanted to get rid of the special prisoners, *schnell*. Some who were considered as less essential were often taken outside and shot out of the frustration to losing the war.

Making the paper for the money was the most difficult of all the tasks. Authentic pounds sterling were prepared from tissue, which the prisoners found to be impossible to replicate. Then, one day, by accident, a counterfeiter took an ordinary dirty rag to use to replicate the paper used by the British. And it worked!

As it turned out, the British made their paper from dirty tissue, but the fastidious Nazis were bringing clean tissue from Turkey. Therein lay the discrepancy. When they finally did learn to make the paper, everything was fine. They made bills amounting to 133 million pounds sterling—40 percent of Britain's money supply. Why So Much Counterfeit Money? The Nazis were trying to destroy the British economy with counterfeit money.

The Nazis divided the counterfeit pounds into three categories. The first were perfect counterfeits. Germany used the *Category I* counterfeit currency to make payments at banks in Switzerland and Scandinavia.

Even the Bank of England approved the counterfeits as being *original*. At the time, pounds sterling were unique in that they were very big: 13 cm by 21 cm. They weren't carried in wallets, but rather attached by a pin to the inside of the pocket so they wouldn't fall out.

Sabotaging the saboteurs—the counterfeiters had their own methods of sabotage. To prevent all the pounds from ending up in circulation, the counterfeiters poked holes through the portrait of the British monarch. Since the British didn't do that, the British took those bills out of circulation.

If all the counterfcit pounds had ended up in circulation in Britain, the economy would have collapsed, which is what the Germans were hoping and striving for.

The threat to the British economy was so extensive, that England requested that the counterfeit pounds in circulation go unmentioned at the Nirenberg trials. A couple years after the war, Britain changed all its bills up to five pounds. It was only then that the danger to the economy disappeared.

That was the first category of counterfeited bills. The second category was comprised of flawed bills where the defects were only visible to specialist. For whatever reason, the German government used them to pay German agents in Europe. The agents didn't realize they were getting paid with fake money until they tried to use it. They typically ended up paying for it with their lives.

The third category had noticeable imperfections. The Germans air dropped this defective currency above English towns, hoping that the English would find and use them to purchase goods, further damaging the British economy.

****

The Nazi-operated workshops counterfeited not only pounds sterling, they made almost everything that could be made from paper: stamps, Soviet rubles, Soviet documents.

Once, they had to falsify 200 identity cards of the Soviet People's Commissariat Security employees. As it turns out, they had purchased the wrong color of red leather. It was much too bright to ever pass inspection.

Kruger accepted no excuses. He insisted that if the cards were not completed in two days, 10 men would be taken out and shot.

They were desperate to save their friends. The resourceful prisoner counterfeiters devised the ingenious idea to use the benches in the barracks.

Their upholstery was a red leatherette, the exact color as needed for the project. They stamped the initials for the Soviet People's Commissariat Security on them and then made covers for the identity cards. Again, they had managed to save the lives of the other prisoners.

****

Stamps! In addition to money, the Bernhard prisoners also counterfeited English postal stamps. They substituted stamps with portraits of Stalin and a six-pointed star for the king's portrait. The fake was intended to create anger among the British towards Jews and Communists.

At first, when the German agents in England glued the stamps on envelopes instead of using genuine stamps, the workers paid little attention. The Nazis plan to trigger hatred towards the Communists and Jews by using stamps with portraits of Stalin and a six-pointed star backfired. The Brits despised the Nazis more.

Chapter 33

When satisfied with the quality and quantity of the British Sterling Pound, the Nazis moved on to instructing the prisoners to counterfeit the American dollar. This assignment caused consternation among the counterfeiters. There were those who realized that if they rebelled against the latest project, their lives, *which were all they had*, would be lost.

Others in the group argued for principal. They felt that if sacrificing themselves was necessary to prevent the counterfeiting of American currency, a deed which would allow the now bankrupt German nation to continue to fight, then so be it.

Again Kruger threatened to take men out and shoot them if sabotage efforts against this project continued. At the very last moment, to save the lives of their comrades, the counterfeiters produced American currency so perfect that Kruger himself deemed them to be a masterpiece. But their production came too late. The allies had Berlin surrounded; the war was ending.

The delays the prisoners created had prevented German access to counterfeit American currency in time for them to save the Nazi war effort. In the last days of the war, the counterfeiting prisoners were instructed to dismantle the printers and pack them up, ready to be moved to isolated mountain caves, where operations would continue. Instead, they seemed to have landed at the bottom of a lake.

Then one day in 1945, first the guards, and then the prisoners, just left.

What Happened to Kruger? Nothing happened to Bernard Kruger, although guilty for the deaths of many prisoners. He was never tried. He died after living many prosperous years in the Federal Republic of Germany, no doubt using some of the expertly crafted counterfeit money to continue his luxurious life style.

So much for the saying, w*hat goes around comes around.*

What happened to the money? Nazis and Nazi sympathizers had retreated to the Austrian Alps intending to fight a last-ditch guerrilla battle. They dumped the currency in the lake to prevent its discovery.

These last ditch activities explain the discarding by the Nazis of the money, along with the printing presses and safes containing information. They landed at the bottom of Lake Toplitz in Austria.

Expeditions trying to find the remnants of the counterfeiting operations as well as other treasures were very dangerous enterprises. They resulted in the death of several people.

In 1963 the Austrian government imposed a ban on explorations in Toplitz after yet another diver, led to the lake by an SS officer, drowned during an illegal dive.

More recent expeditions have had mixed fortunes. In 1983 a German biologist accidentally discovered more forged British pounds, numerous Nazi-era rockets and missiles that had crashed into the lake.

This same biologist also discovered a previously unknown worm. Kudos to the worm for having survived in the midst of all the polluting plunders dumped into the lake. Perhaps it eats antiquated paper currency!

The last diving team to explore the lake in 2000 had even less luck. After a three-week search in an underwater diving capsule, they came away with nothing more than a box full of beer tops. A local fraternity had dumped those into the lake as a practical joke.

Kids!

Chapter 34

The famous treasure hunter, Mr. Spotte, was most recently searching for gold coins. These were thought to be aboard a steamer that had sunk on the way to Panama. Spotte said he was confident he would find "something damn big" in Toplitz.

A Swiss news magazine quoted him as saying, "Until now nobody has explored the lake using hi-tech equipment. We will be the first people to go to the right spot."

A chipper 72 (*hmm – old and rich*), the treasure hunter claims to have discovered fresh clues in the archives in both Berlin and Washington, and these have pointed him towards the gold, though he refuses to provide more details.

Some experts believe he may be right. Because the bottom of the lake is encrusted with a thick carpet of logs, any treasure could be stuck in the mud underneath.

Others who are not so optimistic have pointed out the vast amounts of wood down there. It may not be possible to get through it. The last lot who went down there with a mini U-boat didn't find a thing.

****

Despite all the frustrating failures experienced by search crews, the never ending numbers of treasure hunters remain hopeful. Some vigorous individuals continue to believe that Lake Toplitz, or others like it in Austria or Germany, still hold millions in gold.

The thirst for success and optimism was reignited with the 2003 finding of the Chiemsee Cauldron. Unwavering optimism served this diver well. The diver resurfaced from Lake Chiemsee with a solid gold cauldron decorated with Celtic and Indo-Germanic figures.

Specialists speculate that a top Nazi official, drawing his inspiration from mythology, commissioned the creation of this treasure, later dubbed the Chiemsee cauldron. The cauldron, weighing in at 23 pounds, was valued at $100,000 in 2003.

Chapter 35

I had missed both lunch and dinner. My stomach was growling. Even though starving, I was remiss to venture outside of my cabin in a quest for food. Such an outing would either risk running into and being recognized by the Slarls. Or it would involve clambering back into my disguise. Neither circumstance appealed to me.

My costume was stunning. It consisted of a pink on pink Mumu, under which I strapped a pillow to my waist. I then donned a large floppy hat and dark tortoise shell sunglasses. Although, at the rate I was ordering room surface, I could soon scrap the pillow.

Rather than subject myself to the extravagant efforts of redressing, I again ordered room service—veal stew with a dumpling and a glass of tomato juice. Per usual, my abhorrence of the way animals are raised and slaughtered caused me to eat just the dumpling.

The treasure stories I had been researching were captivating, but I became determined to focus on my original quest—the stamps. Soon, we would approach Austria. Tomorrow I would begin preparations to disembark and explore the Lünersee Lake region.

It then struck me: I had seen neither hide nor hair of the Slarls for at least 12 hours. It's not unusual for honeymooners to spend prolonged periods in their cabin, but I had not seen them at recent meals or in the bars.

A horrible thought struck me. Had they slipped off the boat at the last port? Perhaps they fell overboard? In addition to reassuring myself that they were still on board, I needed to learn more about their plans.

If tragedy had befallen them, perhaps I was earmarked for that same fate. Or perhaps I was to be set up as the prime suspect. I fretted. I should never have let them out of my sight.

On a more personal note, it was troubling not to have heard more about S-woman's reaction to my perfume creation. I had assumed the shrieking heard earlier was the result of slut-woman using the perfume, but that was sheer speculation. Feeling very suspicious and consumed with a bizarre concern for their welfare, I rapped on the adjoining door. I needed to unburden my anxieties. I needed to hear calming reassuring words from Arturo and Saul.

No answer. I tried rapping again, louder this time. Still no answer! I turned the knob. The door swung open to reveal a dark and empty room. There was no evidence of life or luggage. It was as if no one had occupied the room for several days. Entering to take a closer look, I spotted a poster lying on the bed. Perhaps a clue?

THE CLUE?

NINE DAYS OF STAMPS, SAILING & FUN
DESTINATION: SPAIN AND THE CANARY ISLANDS

JOIN THE APS AS WE CRUISE ROUND-TRIP FROM
BARCELONA
WITH STOPS IN SPAIN AND THE CANARY
ISLANDS...EXPLORING, ENJOYING, RELAXING,
SHOPPING...AND VISITING STAMP-ISSUING PORTS-OF-CALL
ABOARD THE
NORWEGIAN CRUISE LINE'S *NORWEGIAN SPIRIT*
VISITING THESE EXCITING, EXOTIC PORTS-OF-CALL:

FUNCHAL, MADEIRA, SANTA CRUZ DE TENERIFE &
ARRECIFE (LANZAROTE), CANARY ISLANDS, GRANADA
(MALAGA), SPAIN

CRUISE HIGHLIGHTS:
FOUR NEW PORTS-OF-CALL
STAMP AUCTION AT SEA
SPECIAL GIFTS
GUEST SPEAKERS
PRIVATE COCKTAIL PARTY

CALL THIS NUMBER FOR RESERVATIONS
860-230-8888

Well, what do you know? Saul and Arturo must be developing a keen interest in philately. Why else would they want to book passage on another philately cruise? The event was still several months away. I was hopeful that we would locate the stamps and develop other interests before then.

Perhaps their resounding confidence that we were on the brink of finding the stamps motivated them to consider the cruise. It would provide an opportunity to do a little trading.

Now, I was worried. Those stamps, should we find them, were not ours to trade. The three of us were going to have a serious discussion.

While waiting for lunch, I vowed to peruse the ship's decks. Maybe the missing parties were still lurking about. I was hopeful that I was not the sole survivor on some weird ghost ship.

Chapter 36

Not all exciting individuals emerging from World War II were adventurers, treasure seekers, or spies. Some were humanitarians!

I was prompted by this next story to remember that having values is more important than having *valu*ables. We were our own style of humanitarians. We would return the stamps, when found.

Raoul Wallenberg was a real life humanitarian. A Swedish diplomat in Nazi-occupied Hungary, he led an extensive and successful mission to save the lives of nearly 100,000 Hungarian Jews.

Wallenberg reached the Swedish delegation in Budapest in July 1944. The campaign against the Jews of Hungary had been underway for several months.

Between May and July 1944, Eichmann and his associates had deported over 400,000 Jews by freight train. Of those deported, all but 15,000 were sent to the Auschwitz-Birkenau concentration camp in southern Poland.

By the time Wallenberg arrived, a mere 230,000 Jews remained in Hungary. He worked with fellow Swedish diplomat, Per Anger. Together, they strove to save Hungarian Jews from additional arrest, deportation, and death.

To do so, Wallenberg issued *protective passports* (German: *Schutz-Pass*). These documents identified the bearers as Swedish subjects awaiting repatriation. They were all that stood between the Jews and deportation.

Although they were not legal, these documents looked official and were generally accepted by German and Hungarian authorities. They were even more appealing when accompanied by a bribe.

The bigger the bribe, the better. The Swedish legation in Budapest also succeeded in negotiating with the German authorities so that those with the protective passes would be treated as Swedish citizens and would be exempt from wearing the yellow badge required for Jews.

With money raised from brave humanitarians, Wallenberg rented at least 32 buildings in Budapest. He declared them to be extraterritorial, and so, protected by diplomatic immunity.

He hung signs, like *The Swedish Library* and *The Swedish Research Institute* on their doors. He suspended oversize Swedish flags on the front of the buildings in an effort to bolster the deception. The buildings came to house almost 10,000 people.

Sandor Ardai, one of the drivers working for Wallenberg, recounted Wallenberg's activities when he intercepted a trainload of Jews about to leave for Auschwitz,

"He climbed up on the roof of the train and began handing in protective passes through the doors which were not yet sealed. He ignored the Germans who were ordering him to get down.

"Then the men from Arrow Cross, the national socialist party, began shooting and shouting at him to go away. Ignoring them, he calmly continued handing out passports to the hands that were reaching out for them."

One might speculate that the Arrow Cross men deliberately aimed over his head. Not one shot hit him, which would have been impossible otherwise. Perhaps they were in awe of his courage, wishing they had but a smidgen of it.

After Wallenberg had handed over the last of the passports, he directed those who had received one to leave the train and walk to get in one of the caravan of cars marked with Swedish colors parked nearby. He saved dozens off that train.

The Germans and Arrow Cross were so dumbfounded, they let him get away. Or, perhaps because Sweden was a neutral country, they were unsure how to react.

At the height of the program, more than 350 people were involved with Wallenberg in the rescue of Jews. Swiss diplomat Carl Lutz joined the efforts to issue protective passports from the Swiss embassy in the spring of 1944.

Italian businessman Giorgio Perlasca posed as a Spanish diplomat and issued forged visas. Berber Smit, the director of N.V. Philips Budapest and a Dutch spy working for the British MI5, also assisted Wallenberg. According to Berber Smit's son, she had had a romance with Wallenberg.

A French nun helped house Jewish women. She was later executed. To avoid capture or being killed by the Arrow Cross members or Adolph Eichmann's men, Wallenberg started sleeping in a different house each night.

Two days before the Russians occupied Budapest, Wallenberg negotiated with both Eichmann and Major-General Gerhard Schmidthüber, the supreme commander of German forces in Hungary.

Wallenberg accomplished this by bribing an Arrow Cross Party member to deliver a note to the occupying Germans. In this note, Wallenberg persuaded the occupying Germans to put a halt to the Fascist plan to blow up the Budapest ghetto. This act would have killed an estimated 70,000 Jews.

He also persuaded them to cancel a final effort to organize a death march of the remaining Jews in Budapest. What leverage did he use to accomplish all of this? The Germans backed off in reaction to his threats to have them prosecuted for war crimes once the war was over.

Wallenberg survived the Nazis, but not the Soviets. Tragedy in the form of the Soviet authorities caught up with this heroic man. On January 17, 1945, during the Siege of Budapest by the Red Army, the Soviets detained Walsenburg on "suspicion of espionage", a trumped-up charge, to be sure. And so he disappeared. Later reports indicate that he died on July 17, 1947 while imprisoned in Lubyanka.

Lubyanka was a palatial building in Moscow, which served as headquarters for the KGB and its affiliated prison. Secrecy and speculation continue to surround Wallenberg's arrest and death, as well as his possible ties to US intelligence.

Wallenberg, remembered for carrying out heroic ideals with non-violent courage, has been honored around the world with countless monuments and statues. Several countries have awarded him honorary citizenship.

The treasures Wallenberg had helped to preserve were human lives.

Chapter 37

S-woman, Karl's new wife, is fairly tall, perhaps a stately 5'8", which seems very tall from my 5'2" perspective. Like me, she is blonde. Perhaps *her* color results from a little help from a bottle, but, whatever. In addition, she has blue eyes. And our similarity ends there.

Slut-woman is voluptuous, a fact that she flaunts by revealing her cleavage with plunging necklines, push-up bras, or no bra whatsoever over skin-tight sweaters. She has sex appeal.

The following tidbit, which I would share with Arturo and Saul if I could find them, was uncovered through my research efforts. It gave me pause when regarding slut-woman's heritage, identity, and intentions.

During the summer of 1942, Wehrmacht soldiers at the bombed-out railroad station in the Ukrainian city of Poltava witnessed a very unusual-looking military unit marching towards a waiting passenger train.

The unit consisted of blonde, blue-eyed women between the ages of 15 and 24, some, perhaps, as young as fourteen. In addition to their striking fairness, they were tall and slender. They wore arresting uniforms that enhanced their already sensational figures and azure eyes.

Each uniform included an Italian-style garrison cap, an A-line skirt with the hem below the knee, and a form-fitting jacket with the insignia of the SS.

One might have thought the SS had recruited a platoon of high-class call girls. Now, why did this description bring to mind the image of S-woman? Because she fit the physical portrayal to a *T*.

Perhaps she is a little younger than the women described would be today, but perhaps not. She may have had cosmetic surgery to keep her true age at bay. Or she may be a descendent. Someone having genetic ties, as well as having been indoctrinated in the Nazi ways of her predecessors.

If Mindy Slutkowski were one of the Ukrainians recruited by the SS, or associated with them in some way, it is Karl who may be in trouble. She could be an active member of *Odessa*. She could just be using Karl to access the stamps and other treasures, hoping to help finance the resurrection of the Nazi movement. I was quite certain that there was something odd and distrustful about her.

****

Further description indicated that these exceptional-looking women from the Ukraine were the result of one of Himmler's brainstorms. He was creating an Antarctic Settlement Women or ASF.

The story actually began in 1938, when the German seaplane carrier, *Schwabenland,* sailed across the South Atlantic. It was bound for Queen Maud's Land in Antarctica.

The following events were reported by the Russian Konstantin Ivanenko, a leading expert in ufology the study of unidentified flying objects—a sterling endorsement, indeed. Keep an open mind. He may not have been completely crazy. According to Ivanenko,

"The Schwabenland sailed to Antarctica, commanded by a veteran of cold-weather operations. The expedition's scientists used their large seaplanes to explore the polar wastes, emulating Admiral Byrd's efforts a decade earlier."

German scientists discovered ice-free lakes that were heated by underground volcanic features and were able to land on them. It is believed that this expedition was aimed at scouting out a secret base of operations in the Antarctica.

During that trip, a German base was established in the mountains just inland from the Princess Astrid Coast. The Germans renamed the area *Neuschwabenland* (New Swabia). The base itself was known only as Station 211.

According to some theories, killing Jews was not the Nazis' main concern. Hitler and the SS were every bit as ruthless, greedy, and power hungry as were the conquerors from ancient times: Genghis Khan and Alexander the

Great. They sought to expand their empires by shuffling large numbers of people around against their will.

In this case, the quest was for a more perfect Aryan race. This reorganization was accomplished through a little-known office of the SS called the *Race and Settlement Bureau* or *Rusha*.

In the Ukraine alone, *Rusha* drafted 500,000 women for forced labor in the munitions factories of Nazi Germany. Of the 500,000 recruits, those who were blonde, blue-eyed, tall, and voluptuous were considered acceptable. Only they would be considered for the platoon of genetic good-lookers, or the Antarctic Settlement of S-women.

Half of these *recruits* were *Volksdeutsch*, that is, ethnic Germans whose ancestors had settled in the Ukraine in the Seventeenth and Eighteenth Centuries. The other half was comprised of native Ukrainians who had been Germanized—upgraded to full Aryan status, as a result of their specific physical attributes.

Ivanenko told us that there was increasing popularity for the idea of a *German-Slavonic Antarctic Reich*. As the story goes, 10,000 of the *racially most pure* Ukrainians were transported to the German Antarctic bases during World War II. The lopsided proportions were four Ukrainian women to one German man.

This was not quite as good of a ratio as 70 virgins to one Muslim martyr, but then again the Germans merely had to survive the Russian front. They were not required to blow themselves to smithereens. Approximately 2,500 German men, who had comprised the Waffen-SS soldiers, were transferred to Station 211 in the Antarctica.

Chapter 38

A training camp that was a combination of finishing school and boot camp was set up on an Estonian island in the Baltic Sea. Here, the chosen Ukrainian women learned an eclectic combination of skills that included exuding charm while freezing.

They practiced accessorizing a parka with seal-skin boots. They performed miscellaneous igloo-keeping duties in addition to Arctic survival and warfare skills. They learned to be seductive while wearing combat boots.

Those who rebelled against the camp were sent to and terminated in Auschwitz. One identifiable case of rebellion occurred in 1943. An Auschwitz guard, Irma Greese, age 22 and the periodic girl friend of the infamous Dr. Josef Mengele, took to wearing a sky-blue ASF uniform.

She had scavenged this uniform from a pile of discarded inmate clothing. Turns out, the uniform belonged to a Ukrainian recruit who had preferred being sent to Auschwitz over being sent to the Antarctica to become an ice whore.

On a side note: Greese, the guard, was hanged in 1946 for war crimes. That uniform brought bad luck to all who wore it.

Himmler used large, obsolete-style German submarines, almost as large as tramp steamers, to cart supplies and personnel to Antarctica. His rationale for sending thousands of settlers to the frozen wasteland might be understood within the context of his mystic beliefs.

Himmler had become a believer in the Hindu concept of world-ages or *Yugas*. He believed that the current age, *Kali Yuga*, would end in a global cataclysm, giving birth to a new world-age, *Satya Yuga*.

To be more concise, the Antarctic settlement was Himmler's attempt to preserve the Arian race despite any cataclysmic events.

Chapter 39

One can assimilate an amazing amount of information by being a good listener in a pub, café, or *biergarten*, depending upon the country. This is especially true when one freely pays for rounds of drinks.

I always made certain to enter such an arena after the drinking was already underway, but not yet to an extreme. Under those conditions, fewer drinks or pitchers are required to prime still lucid conversation.

On my last trip to the continent, I had pulled a chair up to a table where an older man sat with comrades.

Don't be alarmed. It's traditional to share tables in Europe.

They made me feel quite welcome, more so when I ordered another pitcher of beer for all to enjoy. One of the stories I heard from this elderly gent, whose name I came to learn was Dieter, was fascinating.

He described himself as a small boy growing up during the Second World War,

"Even as a little boy, I knew enough to keep away from the old salt mine in Wansleben am See. The only hint of what was going on inside came when the gaunt prisoners wearing blue-striped uniforms arrived under SS guard to collect bread from the bakery. We were told they were bad people; that they were enemies of Germany. Stay away from them. They had to be locked up."

His friend, who had shared his age as being 74, said,

"It was forbidden to talk about the mine and the prisoners while at school."

The salt mine, *Wansleben am See*, was hiding one of the final secrets of the Nazis. It was not until 60 odd years after the war that documents found in the archive of East Germany's secret police, the Stasi, revealed how the Nazis used a vast subterranean complex as a concentration camp.

A retired pit foreman, Herr Horst, stumbled on evidence while researching the local history of the mining industry.

He reviewed documents revealing that more than 1,500 prisoners worked among its tunnels and caverns. Many died.

Rather than mining, the SS had their workers use secret tunnels linking the two mine shafts for storing treasures in the form of rare books, priceless paintings and letters by Goethe. Everything described in these documents has vanished, but the mines also had other uses. Survivors have shared their stories,

> Workers from other camps, including Buchenwald, were brought to the site in 1944 to carve out vast underground chambers. Safe from allied bombers, production equipment was lowered into the mines where the Polish, French, Russian, and even some Jewish, workers assembled parts for Germany's war industry.

A former French resistance fighter who survived the war revealed,

> There were three eight hour shifts, 6am-2pm, 2-10pm and 10pm-6am. We slept above ground in bunks. Being underground while we worked protected us from the cold. As in caves, the temperature was constant, but perhaps a little warmer than a cave's ambient temperature—(50F). No one could ever escape. One of my French friends tried, but when he was captured three days later and brought back to the camp, he was hanged along with two Russians who had attempted to flee with him. And we all had to watch. Even so, the camp was not as terrible as some of the others. We weren't exterminated, but were kept alive in a healthy enough state so that we could work.

But by March and April 1945 there was less and less to eat. The Germans had nothing to give the prisoners. The soup was nothing more than watery gruel.

Letters from inmates found in the Stasi archive paint an even grimmer picture. According to a former Polish prisoner, named Stanislaus,

> We worked in the gloom with open wounds. Those too ill to work disappeared. Their bodies were cremated nearby. Many of the raw materials used to make weapons came

from churches looted by the Nazis. There were crucifixes, candelabras, chalices, and candlesticks, all made from gold and silver.

On April 11 1945, with allied forces closing in, SS guards forced surviving prisoners to leave the camp. According to Clauss, another former inmate 84 years of age,

> It was a death march. Those who couldn't walk were shot by the side of the road. Between 50 and 70 of my comrades were killed.

Claus managed to escape, but another SS patrol recaptured him. The patrol decided to execute him. An SS officer shot him in the head. Amazingly, he survived, waking up hours later to discover the bullet had passed through his ear and jaw. He was left with a huge headache and a gaping wound in his jaw. The village grocer hid him when he returned to town.

The Americans liberated the village the following day. Claus, who still lives in the village and still has a headache, recalled,

> After the Americans came, prisoners came knocking on our door asking for clothes. My mother gave them some underpants. They were extremely thin. A few days prior, an SS commandant had stolen my father's car in an attempt to escape.

The underground camp's existence was swiftly forgotten as US investigators concentrated on another camp in nearby Nordhausen. There, the Americans found sensational diagrams of Hitler's secret V2 rocket.

Another underground facility held in storage the entire collection of rare 16th- and 17th-century medical and botanical books. The books were from Germany's most famous scientific academy, the Leopoldina.

The Russians arrived 11 weeks after the Americans. They took the entire collection of more than 7000 books and thirteen oil paintings, back to Moscow.

In the 1960s East Germany's communist regime launched a secret investigation into the mine. A Stasi investigator reported,

> Inside, they found a postcard from 15-year-old child, probably of Jewish origin. There were also several sacks full of SS documents. There was not one sign of the precious books and paintings. The mine was sealed once again shortly afterwards.

To this day, only 50 books from the vanished collection have been returned to the library from which they came. The rest are believed to still be in Russia. The library received a few things back from the Georgians, but nothing from the Russians.

There is little to identify the old mine as a former Nazi camp. Above ground there are few clues, but one would have to be well familiar with the history of the region to pick them out.

All that remains from that era is a cobbled street where the prisoners marched, a few outbuildings, and a railway cutting that is overgrown with brush, brambles and fruit trees. There is no monument.

The historical society of the region would like to erect a memorial, but has little money. There is a monument in the village square, erected under the communist region, commemorating those who were victimized by fascism.

The rest of the world may have forgotten these underground prisons and labor camps, but the few surviving prisoners had not forgotten their atrocious experiences. This was evidenced when one of the camp overseers, who had fled after the war, later returned.

He was recognized by one of the surviving Polish prisoners. That particular former camp overseer was found riddled with bullets, Perhaps each bullet honored one of the inmate's friends who had died at this man's hand.

****

My cell phone began to vibrate.

Hot dog! Communication!

Any distraction was welcome at this point. I didn't recognize the number, so considered letting voice mail intercept it. But, if the other party did not leave a message, then I would never know who had called. The number displayed as unknown. Besides, I was desperate to talk to someone, anyone.

By the time I finished discussing the situation with myself, the result of spending too much alone time, the phone had stopped vibrating. The tale-tale beep of a message being left sounded. Problem solved.

I dialed into my voice mail. All I could hear was some frantic yelling and cursing. Then the message cut off.

Had the Slarls *called me by mistake?*

Chapter 40

I spent the next several hours preparing to disembark from the philatelic cruise ship. I had resigned myself to reinitiating the stamp quest alone. I had not a clue where Saul and Arturo were.

Traveling lightly has its advantages. I stuffed everything into my backpack, including my laptop. In twenty or so minutes, the boat would be docking in Durnstein, Austria.

Having performed a quick *MapQuest* search, I groaned in disappointment, realizing that I had undershot. To reach the Lünersee region, I would have to drive southwest. The trip would take approximately 5.75 hours. At least no one would be expecting me so far off the mark.

My immediate need, once going ashore, was to find an English speaking person who could direct me to a car rental agency. I stepped into an elevator near my cabin.

Determined not to be crushed into a corner by thirty other passengers as eager as I to reach shore, I pounded on the *Close Door* button (> <). I hoped to be long gone before others appeared.

Just when I thought I had it made, a skinny withered arm reached through. The door abruptly reversed the closing process. The wizened arm was followed by a very, very thin older woman.

She stepped in with exaggerated deliberation while glaring at me through cold, piercing eyes. The look displayed such ferocity and unbridled disgust that I had to look away. How odd and unnerving! I must admit to being completely nonplussed by her obvious detestation. I was the recipient of hatred from a complete stranger.

Or was she?

Just then my phone rang providing a merciful distraction from my intimidating elevator companion. It was Saul calling to tell me that he and Karl had secured a car and would be waiting in the dock's parking lot. A sense of renewed courage and relief washed over me.

I was just a little perplexed over how they knew where I would be disembarking. But, nevertheless, I sauntered down the ramp to the dock, feeling as though a heavy weight had been lifted from my shoulders.

Good gosh! There they were, waving like mad men. I first spotted Saul's long red scarf with fringe even longer than I had remembered. Next I spotted Arturo, a rolled cigarette hanging out of the side of his mouth, looking happier than he had in weeks.

What a welcome sight! I rushed over and threw my arms around the two, delighted to once again have human contact and overwhelmed by their obvious display of happiness at seeing me. So much for my unanticipated and discreet exit from the ship at that port!

"Um," Saul said,

"Don't get too carried away. Arturo is smiling because he's just had an offer for his magazine... a nice round seven-figure number."

"Oh," I said somewhat taken aback,

"That's, that's just awesome news, Arturo."

While I was happy for Arturo, I suspected that the sale of the magazine might mean that unemployment loomed in my future.

Arturo jumped in,

"And they want me to stay on as managing editor and for you to be a staff editor!"

Well, well, perhaps this was good news.

"Who is purchasing the magazine," I inquired.

"And what will my salary be. I will be salaried, right, with benefits like healthcare, vacation, sick days?"

Then I cautioned,

"One can't be too careful! There are companies out there that buy out smaller companies, borrow against them, and then, after accruing huge amounts of debt in their name, declare bankruptcy. And the newly purchased company is left stuck with the financial burden."

Having dampened everyone's good humor and dreams of unparalleled wealth, I crawled into the backseat of the rented car secured by Saul and Arturo. But, instead of heading southwest towards the Lünersee, I noticed that we were heading northwest towards the Frankfurt airport.

I was so tense that I failed to notice that Arturo and Saul had been talking non-stop. They were chattering something about research, the Antarctica, Nova Scotia, coyotes, and Newfoundland. All while they were heading towards the Frankfurt airport.

This can't be happening again.

I was astounded. I needed to get to that damned lake. I couldn't let them hijack this trip. We were too close to *the destination* not to proceed to Lake Lünersee.

I calmed down long enough to listen to Saul and Arturo describing their most recent research interest. These two have become even more fascinated with microbes. According to them, a remarkable event occurred in 1999 that never received the attention it deserved.

Remember that Saul had brought Froggy, the tiny antibiotic producing amphibian with him on this trip. How is Froggy relevant?

In 1999, a research expedition discovered a virus in Antarctica *that was virulent to people and animals.* At the time, the discovery was ignored. The thinking was that a virus in the Antarctica was much too far away to be of concern to the rest of the world's population.

With the threat of global warming, the viral discoveries take on new importance. Once the icecaps melt and the permafrost disappears, the viruses will be waiting for a live, warm body to invade to begin reproducing.

There was the possibility that the discovered virus may be just one of many. Unimaginable catastrophes may be awaiting us once the thaw is underway.

American scientists have taken the Antarctic discovery seriously and have organized expeditions to test the ice. They're searching for additional viruses so that they have time to develop vaccines and antidotes before any major pandemics strike.

Too bad they were viruses. We have a great source for an antibacterial antibiotic, eh Froggy!

What is the source of these viruses in the land where the penguin rules? Several theories exist. The two most prominent are: 1) these life forms survived in the permafrost, and 2) the Germans secretly delivered a biological weapon to the Antarctic.

This last concept arose not in a vacuum. It is known that the Nazis became interested in Antarctica as early as 1938. They organized expeditions to the area in 1938-1939.

The Nazi explorers first dropped colored pennants from airplanes. They then named the area *Neuschwabenland*. As far as they were concerned, it was now a part of the New Reich.

While we sped along in our Volkswagen, Saul shared the following,

"In 1943, Germany's submarine fleet was proud of the 'unassailable fortress it had created for the Führer on the other end of the world.' The Nazis were building a secret base in the Antarctica during the years between 1938 and 1943.

"Submarines were the chosen mode of transportation for the necessary freight heading for those cold nether regions. Specialists indicated that submarines were relieved of their rockets to make room for the containers of different goods.

"Even more intriguing was the fact that passengers with faces swathed in bandages were seen boarding the submarines. Either Nazis were obscuring their identity with fake bandages or they had undergone plastic surgery in an attempt to flee without capture."

I sat there chortling, imagining a German colony where all the former Nazis looked twenty years younger and identical to each other. Much the way older Hollywood stars who have *undergone the knife* do.

****

In 1945, one of these submarines, the Valkyrie-2, left the port in Kiel. Upon arriving in the Antarctica, sixteen members of the crew dug an ice cave and stored the containers it transported in the cave. As legend has it, the boxes contained relics of the third Reich, including Hitler's personal documents. Perhaps they included a secret cache of deadly virus, and, maybe, more stolen valuables—like gold, and jewels.

On July 10, 1945, the operation concluded. The submarine entered the Argentinean port of Mar-del-Plata and surrendered to the authorities.

Another submarine, another premise: This submarine, under the command of Heinz Schäffer, reputedly delivered *the remains of Adolf Hitler and Eva Braun* to *Neuschwabenland*. It followed the route of the U-530 submarine and arrived at Mar-del-Plata, Antarctica, on August 17, 1945.

The submarines captains were interrogated by the American and British intelligence services. They revealed that the submarines delivered relics to the Antarctica shores. Their admissions seem dubious. It is unlikely that such a serious operation was designed only for the sake of delivering Third Reich documents and relics.

Later, special services seized a confidential letter of Captain Schäffer, from the submarine, to his friend, Captain Wilhelm Bernhard, of counterfeiting fame. It appeared that Bernhard planned to publish his memoirs.

The letter was dated June 01, 1983 and reads as follows:

Dear Willy,

I was thinking if it is reasonable to publish your manuscript concerning the submarine activity to the Antarctica. The three submarines that took part in that operation (U-977, U-530 and U-465) are currently at the bottom of the Atlantic Ocean. Isn't it better to leave them there? My old friend, think about it! Think please how then my book will look when you publish your memoirs.[1] We all made an oath to keep the secret; we did nothing wrong, we just obeyed the orders and fought for our loved Germany and its survival. Please think again: isn't it better to picture everything as a fable? What results do you plan to achieve with your revelations? Think about it, please.

---

[1] After WWII, Heinz Schäffer wrote a book, entitled *U-977*.

Even 40 years after the events, Heinz insisted that Bernhard must resist revealing the truth. Did the submarines indeed deliver something more dangerous to the continent, not just Hitler's documents or stolen treasures?

****

On December 30, 1946, a U.S. Navy patrol plane with a crew of nine, mapping the Antarctic coast as part of a military effort called Operation High Jump crashed in a snowstorm after its radar failed to detect a slope not shown on the charts.

The U.S. Navy, piggybacking on scientific explorations of western Antarctica, had begun efforts to locate the plane and recover the remains of the crew members who died.

There are expectations that, in addition to the crew, they may be successful in finding the fabled German sub-icicle colony comprised of *über* Ukrainians and Germans. It may be a lot easier with global warming. Not as many polar caps to obscure visibility.

Chapter 41

So, I got to thinking about slut-woman again. (I often refer to her as s-woman out of politeness.) If the Antarctic colony were established by the Germans in the '40s, it's very possible that she could be a descendent of one of the original über Antarctic settlers. She could have been implanted into a sleeper cell after receiving training similar to that received by the original settlers.

The recent flurry of activities of other individuals pursuing Nazi treasures caused her cell to be activated. Perhaps her role was to keep close tabs on Karl et al., ensuring that those who came a little too close to the truth would disappear. That could mean that Karl, too, might be in danger, although she did seem somewhat fond of him.

"Elyse, Elyse! Are you awake back there?" Saul's loud query from the front of the car jarred me from my musings.

"I am now," I snapped.

"I'm also hungry. Do you think we can stop somewhere to eat on the way to the airport?"

Arturo said to Saul,

"Let dis be a lesson to you. Never waken de sleeping bear!"

Saul replied,

"I believe that the saying is, *Let sleeping dogs lie.*"

I just snarled.

After we had all eaten and were in better moods, Saul exchanged a glance with Arturo, who gave him a slight nod. He then said,

"Elyse, or are you one of your aliases, Edna or Ethel, today? We have some very serious information we need to share with you."

Let me guess.

"The sunken submarines laden with treasure near the Antarctica and the ship wreck off the coast of Nova Scotia aren't the primary motivation for returning to Newfoundland and Nova Scotia, and then on to Antarctica.

"We weren't certain how or when we should break the news, but now seems as good a time as any. You mentioned you hadn't seen Karl or slut-woman on the cruise ship for the last several days. Is that correct?"

I nodded, not knowing where he was going with this.

Saul continued,

"Since Arturo and I thought we should do a little preliminary scouting around Lünersee, we arranged for one of our Interpol colleagues to follow them."

From a strategic point of view, this was a wise move. If Arturo and Saul showed up in too many of the same scenarios, they might notice. It's to our advantage that they think they are not under surveillance.

Saul went on,

"Well, we just heard back from that colleague. Karl and slut-woman, for some unknown reason, had aborted their plans to go to Lünersee. Instead, they popped up in Nova Scotia—Cape Breton to be precise. This is what they reported,

'While hiking to some unknown destination, they were attacked by a pack of coyotes. Certain coyotes on the Cape are believed to have mated with wolves, producing a hybrid, the Coywolf. For unknown reasons, that species has become very aggressive.

'This hybrid now has the strength and the intelligence of the magnificent wolf. But the wolf's noble qualities are now blended in with the wiliness and deceitfulness of the coyote. The result is a sly, but aggressive, very powerful and intelligent animal.'"

I was holding my breath while waiting for Saul to continue,

"The news is that a couple of backpackers, a man and a woman, were attacked by a trio of these hybrids. The remains of the woman are still unrecovered. The male is rumored to be incommunicado—suffering from shock. The fear is that the female remains are those of the person you so unceremoniously refer to as slut-woman."

"Authorities were able to tentatively identify her because the Slarls had registered at the Rangers Station for this particular hike, but they never signed back in. No one else is deemed missing."

"No," I squealed, not knowing whether to laugh or cry. This situation seemed too bizarre. What an ignominious, horrifying fate.

Arturo picked up where Saul left off,

"It is believed dat de victim was wearing some unusual fragrance dat not only attracted the carnivores, but drove them into a violent frenzy. Dis was our reason for wanting to return to Newfoundland and Nova Scotia. It would make an interesting article for de magazine, and as Interpol agents, we need to ensure dey don't have contraband in der possession."

Trying to hide my guilt, I exclaimed,

"Oh my goodness, it was an unusual fragrance?"

Ouch! What had I called it? Acid Rain? Essence de Froggy?

I couldn't remember.

Saul and Karl were both staring at me.

Well, let them stare. I'm not admitting to anything. It certainly wasn't my intention for her to be eaten. Who even knew they were traveling to Cape Breton?

Since I had covered my tracks well, the enhanced *fragrance* was unlikely to be traced back to me. And I had discarded my oversized dress and padding before leaving the ship. They were now flotsam.

"I'm sorry. I'm just so surprised and upset. I disliked her, but, well, never wished her to die... or die again," I stammered.

I was remembering how she and Karl had tricked us into believing she had fallen to her death into a kiva during a past confrontation in the southwest. Considering that sequence of events, maybe we should remain a tad skeptical. Normal coyotes are very shy animals. Although they have been known to be aggressive around a kill they're trying to protect.

"Okay, Boys, tell me everything you know and how and where you got the information."

Arturo answered first,

"It was on de newswire. Slut-woman, if indeed it was Slut-woman, was walking with Karl on a skyline trail in a national park on Cape Breton. Oder hikers in de area heard de commotion and tried to run de coyotes off, but couldn't. Dey said the animals were in such a frenzied state dat noting scared dem. Dey said dat they tought it was de horrendous odor coming from de woman dat enraged de coyotes, or coywolves, as dey are technically referred to."

"What makes us think it was Slut-woman," I wistfully asked. "What would she and Karl be doing on Cape Breton? And how did Karl escape?"

It was Saul's turn to pick up the thread,

"Colleagues of ours have been tracking them. They saw them leave the cruise ship at some obscure port in Germany. They then flew back to Halifax after receiving a telegram. They were traveling along the coast when the incident took place."

I complained,

"I don't understand any of this. We're supposed to be pursuing the fabled Lünersee stamps, aren't we? And weren't they buried somewhere near Lake Lünersee? Isn't that what we've been led to believe? So why is the focus now on Canada? Unless, Karl and Slut-woman have already recovered the stamps and are now attempting to either re-conceal them in another location or fence them."

After further consideration, I continued,

"What if Karl and slut-woman are once again just pretending that she was killed? And why, again, were the coyotes so frenzied? They're usually very timid around people."

Said Arturo,

"Again, dis is speculation. Autorities teorize dat she was wearing or emitting a very strange odor. Perhaps, de odor was from some sort of cologne or perfume. And dis is what excited them. Speculation is dat it was similar to de musk emitted by a horny, but injured animal. Someone reported seeing her wit a strange pink perfume bottle, but dey were unable to find it with her belongings."

Uh, oh, it's almost certain that the odor was Essence de Froggy.

Arturo continued,

"Because of de mystery surrounding her, Saul and I, using de tools available to us tru Interpol, came up wid dis accounting. You might want to read it."

Saul handed me a semi-thick report.

Chapter 42

I skimmed through the report's pages. In effect, slut-woman's real name was Mindy Slutkowski, of Ukrainian descent. The exact place of her birth is unclear, but in 1990, she married a Brit.

After spending a year in England, the couple immigrated to New Jersey. In 1994, her British husband mysteriously disappeared from a vacation cruise ship. Mindy became quite wealthy as a consequence.

To escape the notoriety surrounding her husband's disappearance, Slutkowski moved to a small rural town in Tennessee. There she kept a low profile for years, working for a small telecommunications company. She only resurfaced on the radar in 2011 when she hooked up with Karl.

This information was a perfect fit to the profile I had created for her. She had to be an über Ukrainian, or the descendent of one.

Saul interjected,

"Having tapped into her computer and perused her emails, it has become obvious to both Interpol and the FBI that she's fluent in Russian, English, French, and German. These are qualities atypical of a low level technology employee."

Arturo added,

"Slut-woman, before marrying Karl, was trying to maintain a low profile. We suspect that she is/was part of a sleeper cell, one of de most insidious tactics used by terrorist organizations."

Sleeper-cell terrorists are difficult to find and the US is particularly vulnerable because of its porous and huge borders. The northern border of the U.S., which it shares with Canada stretches for more than 4,000 miles.

The southern border with Mexico runs about half that length, or 2,000 miles. The next problem is that long stretches of both borders are unpopulated and unpatrolled, making it easy for spies and terrorists to slip through.

Every year some 10,000 immigrants with questionable backgrounds disappear into Canada's ethnic communities. Every year, innumerable immigrants flow from Canada into the US. This and other factors contribute to approximately 12 million living with concealed identities in the continental United States.

A sleeper cell consists of secret agents who received specialized training in their home countries, in this case the Ukraine and Russia. After training completion, the agents are then assigned to assimilate into a country's culture and society. There is no way of knowing the precise number. Hence, the ease with which sleeper cells can become established.

The first husband of Mindy was merely a tool for her to become legally established in the US. Sleeper agents such as Mindy spend years performing normal activities.

During that period, they live in deep undercover, assuming fictitious identities before receiving orders from their overseas handlers. Those orders usually include either committing an act of terrorism or providing aid to those who will.

Individual members of the same sleeper cell may not even be aware of each other. This tactic makes them less vulnerable during police interrogations. This technique is vital to their survival.

For example, one sleeper agent may work for an airline ticket office. Another, like Mindy, will work for a low level telecommunications company.

Yet another agent may work at a car rental company or at a chemical plant. When the commander of a covert organization wants to activate a sleeper cell, each agent may receive just the name of one contact person or just his or her specific orders.

For example, the airline ticket agent may receive instructions to provide tickets for four men traveling from Germany to New York. The car rental agent may be told to provide a car to these men at the airport, or to have someone deliver them discreetly and safely to a nuclear power plant.

Mindy, as an example, may be instructed to use her skills to provide activated, untraceable cell phones for these individuals. This type of strategy would ensure that no individual member of the sleeper cell is aware of the entire plan.

In this specific case, Mindy, most likely, was told to contact and become close to Karl, since he was known to have some connection to the Lünersee stamps. They may also have concluded that he had knowledge of other Nazi treasures from the World War II era.

Saul added,

"We suspect that the motivation for activating Mindy was the revived interest in the precious artifacts stolen during WWII. Russia is still searching for clues to the Amber Room treasure."

"Well, I'll be," I said.

"Having observed her, I would never have guessed she was smart enough to be multi-lingual. I'm impressed."

Saul cautioned,

"Don't be too impressed. She's like a savant who excels at languages and nothing else. What makes her so valuable to the rest of the team is the fact that she, ahem, unlike you, follows orders without ever questioning them. She's like a machine that can be programmed, carrying out her manager's bidding like a well-executed computer program."

"But, then again, she's dead, eaten by coyotes," I mumbled to myself.

Or is she?

I had been scammed twice by slut-woman and Karl into thinking that one, or the other, was dead. Karl had faked his death in my presence by actually swallowing wine laced with cyanide during a scrabble game.

It was only after I had left his premises that Mindy, unbeknownst to me, injected him with the antidote, enabling him to revive and then recover. It had all been planned. Reacting to this scenario, I asked,

"Do you think Karl is aware of her background—that she's a possible descendant from a Ukrainian über-woman? He could be in danger. If she's not dead, that is. Has anyone seen the body?"

"Well, no. That's the problem." Saul admitted.

"Karl, who was with her, claims that her body was dragged away by the coyotes. There were so many that he was 'powerless against them.' So, all authorities have to go on, so far, is his word."

"Well, that's worth its weight in gold," I replied with just a touch of sarcasm.

"I'm quite certain that, if in fact the attack occurred, there would be some evidence."

"Well," said Arturo with his charming accent, "we can't entirely dismiss de possibility. After all, in recent years, der have been several coyote attacks in de area."

He continued to describe a couple stories,

"One teenage woman was actually killed by two coyotes working in tandem with each udder. And two udder teens have been attacked since den. Neider of dem suffered serious wounds. Coyote attacks are a reality in dat part of Nova Scotia.

"Another victim was a young boy riding a dirt bike along a hiking trail. When he got off de bike, he was rushed by a lone coyote, who must have been stalking him over a great distance.

"De other incident involved a young girl walking to school. She heard snarling in the underbrush, but when she didn't see anything, she continued walking. When least expecting it, she was rushed, struck from behind, and knocked over by a lone coyote.

"A passing motorist saw de incident and scared de animal away by blowing his horn. One can only imagine what might have happened if he hadn't happened by and interfered just den!"

"These stories creep me out," I said. "So it is possible that she *is* dead. But how does this affect our search for the stamps? And what were they doing in Nova Scotia? Shouldn't *we* just continue on to Lake Lünersee and pick up the stamp trail, should one exist, and go from there."

Why do we need to follow Karl and s-woman? Maybe they're just trying to confuse us?

Chapter 43

On the subject of lost treasures, Nazis were not the only looters. During WW II, the Japanese were guilty of plundering treasure from at least thirteen Asian countries. They confiscated precious jewels and diamonds, gold bullion and a solid gold Buddha. The Japanese booty never reached the shores of Japan because of the US's naval blockade.

According to Philippines' survivors who had worked with the Japanese royalty and military during this period, much of the loot was buried in tunnels that were constructed in the Philippines for the purpose of hiding treasures.

Towards the end of the war, these tunnels were dynamited. They were planted with explosives that were detonated despite the presence of engineers in them who were inventorying the goods.

A few servants with strong ties to the Japanese princes were warned before the explosions occurred. They were able to escape. Many shared their stories decades later.

Some of the more spectacular treasures included 18 solid gold Buddhas, each weighing approximately 2200 pounds. The only compromise made in their solid gold construction was a small cavity accessed by screwing off the head. It was used to hide precious gems.

A plaintiff against the Marcos government involving the rights to one of these three-foot high Buddhas was awarded $22 billion plus interest. The government had unlawfully confiscated the Buddha he had discovered in a cave.

In 1945, US intelligence officers in Manila discovered that the Japanese had hidden large quantities of gold bullion and other looted treasure in the Philippines. President Truman decided to clandestinely recover that gold.

There were other sources for WW II treasure in addition to the Philippines, Germany, Austria, and Switzerland plunders. There are at least two instances, possibly three, in which British ships carried precious metals and gems from both Russia and England. These riches were to be used as payment to the US for its aid and involvement.

Unfortunately, the ships sank.

One of the ships went down somewhere along the North American coast between Halifax and Cape Cod.

Could the possibility of sunken treasure off the coast of Nova Scotia be the reason for slut-woman's and Karl's new found interest in that area?

Chapter 44

Not all sunken Nazi treasures were concealed in alpine lakes or at the bottom of mine shafts or in caves. There are at least two or three that rest somewhere at the bottom of the ocean.

> *Sunken Treasure # 1*: A record 48-ton haul of silver bullion, worth $38 million, was recovered from a WWII shipwreck off the coast of Ireland by a deep ocean exploration firm. The treasure, worth 1.4 million troy ounces of silver, was found in the wreckage three miles beneath the Atlantic.
> The operation to retrieve the 1,203 bars from the SS Gairsoppa is the heaviest and deepest underwater mission ever to remove precious metal from sunken vessels. The boat carried 83 crew and two gunners, but only one officer managed to reach the shore after the ship was hit by a German torpedo.
>
> *Sunken Treasure #2*: In November 1941, two ships crossed paths off the coast of Australia. One was the German raider *HSK Kormoran*. The other was an Australian battle ship called the *HMAS Sydney*. Guns were fired. Both ships sustained enormous damage and sank.

Australia was especially keen on recovering its own downed ship. The loss of the Sydney was considered a national tragedy. The Australian government also hoped to reclaim the 645 bodies of the sailors, hoping to provide comfort and to bring closure to their families.

Despite extensive search efforts during and after World War II, the ships weren't found until 2008. That is the year that a team of psychologists analyzed the statements from the surviving German crew members.

The 300 surviving German sailors who had abandoned their ship, and were rescued before it sank, provided statements about where they thought the ships had gone down. The problem was, their memories varied so greatly that many thought that they were lying.

A former director of the *Finding Sydney Foundation*, a non-profit group established to help find the Sydney, stated that this memory variance wasn't at all unusual—particularly during wartime.

Knowledge of the ship's position is on a need to know basis and, for the most part, kept in the bridge area. It's not surprising that most sailors would not be privy to that information. They could only estimate the ships' positions.

Some 70 sailors did come up with a location, but the information they provided, when compiled, made little sense when taken at face value. The positions were spread over hundreds of miles. One individual even suggested that the ships went down near the Antarctica.

Enter two psychologists. A cognitive psychologist from the University of Western Australia first became interested in finding the Sydney in the 1990s. After attempting several different approaches to solving the problem, he brought in his friend and frequent collaborator, a cognitive psychologist from the University of Adelaide.

By the time they entered the picture in the mid-to-late 1990s, a myriad of people with innumerable theories had already attempted to find the ships,

If you didn't believe the Germans, the number of possibilities was endless as to what might have happened and where the ships might be. Lots of theories had been expounded and lots of areas had been suggested.

The cycle was always the same: Some treasure hunter with a theory would propose a site. People would rush to look. There would be excitement, followed by disappointment.

Cognitive psychologists took a very different view of the German accounts. To them, the spread of the reports looked like the kind of data they saw in memory experiments. They set about to prove in a scientific manner that the Germans were probably telling the truth,

> *We wanted to make the case. We wanted to show that the characteristics of these reports were the right kind of characteristics.*
> *That is, the inconsistencies in the reports were precisely the kind of inconsistencies that occur naturally from failures of memory and the vagaries of transmitting information from person to person.*

To make this case, they turned to the work of a British psychologist. He, like the other two, was a psychologist interested in what happens to memory over time.

In the 1930s he conducted his now famous experiment with a Native American folk tale called *The War of the Ghosts*. His experiment was much like the American game of telephone, where one person repeats to another a phone message.

That person passes the message onto another, and so on. By the time the message is repeated back to the initiator, it has absolutely no similarity to the original message.

The War of the Ghosts is a very old tale with bizarre sentence construction and unpredictable leaps in the story line.

To test the theory that the memory is faulty (to say the least), the psychologist would read the story aloud to a test subject. Immediately, the subject would repeat what he had heard. He would make a written record of the interpretation.

After a week, or several weeks, the British psychologist would have the subject, or subjects, once again repeat the story and again making a record of their latest interpretation.

Here are the first two sentences that were read to the subjects,

> One night two young men from Egulac went down to the river to hunt seals, and while they were there it became foggy and calm. Then they heard war cries and thought, "Maybe this is a war party."

Here's how test subject *R* recalled the story after first hearing it,

> There were two young men, and they went on the river side. They heard war cries.

Here's how R recalled the same two sentences 14 days later,

> There were ghosts. They went on a river.

The subject of ghosts kept coming up—weird! And the same sentences after a month,

> There were ghosts. There took place a fight between them.

One expects there to be changes in any repeated narrative, but the changes were predictable. In their recall attempts, the subjects tried to have the story make more sense to them by changing the elements.

The fact that the subjects tried to make the story conform to a more traditional narrative made Bartlett theorize that memory is composed of two parts:

> When a memory is formed, the content becomes embedded in a schema, or theory of what is going on. Over time, less of the original content and more of the general theory is remembered.
>
> The basic gist of the story is supplemented or changed to fit a more comfortable mold. According to another experiment by Bartlett, the same pattern of change continues as the story passes from one person to the next.

How do these examples relate to the Germans' theories of where the boats sank? The Australian psychologists decided that the German survivors' reports should be compared directly to the Bartlett experiment.

They took the story versions that Bartlett had documented and counted up all of the changes in them. Every shift in a sentence or a word was noted and recorded in graph form. They were then able to produce a particular statistical profile.

The two psychologists did the exact same thing with the German accounts. They arranged the 70 accounts into groups that seemed to be related to one another, and then charted them on a graph.

Their data, compiled from the German sailor's statements, were very similar to the data generated in the study of the British psychologist. This suggested to the Australian psychologists that the Germans had relayed the events as they remembered them. They were not lying.

It was not a contrived set of data. The variance displayed was the kind of natural variance you get with normal memory loss.

They determined that the Germans were in all probability telling the truth. They sat down with a map of the Indian Ocean and tried to pinpoint the place on the map that best fit the variety of accounts of where the ships had gone down,

To do this, they took each point in the ocean and looked at how well it satisfied or conformed to each of the German's statements.

They then marked a spot as the place where they thought the German ship would be found. In 2004, the two Aussies gave the information to the Finding Sydney Foundation. At that time there were no concrete plans to search for the boats. For all intents and purposes, that was that. They never thought that they would find out whether it would be right or wrong.

But then a funny thing happened. A professional shipwreck hunter convinced the Australian government to let him go searching for the wrecks. In March 2008 he went out and, using his own methods, he discovered the wreck of the German ship.

You may ask,

How far was the ship from the point that the Aussie psychologists had pinpointed four years earlier?

Turns out, their calculation was amazingly accurate.

One of them remarked,

"It was 2.7 nautical miles from the point we put down. Whoa! It worked! I was amazed, actually."

A couple of days after the German ship was found, so, too, was the Australian ship, the Sydney. It had sunk to the bottom of the ocean just a short distance away from the German ship that had attacked it 67 years before.

One wonders if the German ship had been returning from a trip taking supplies and personnel to their secret Antarctica site. This premise was reinforced by a German sailor speculating that their ship had sunk while still in the Antarctic waters.

Chapter 45

"Well, Guys," I said to my two traveling companions,
"From the way it sounds, we can stop just about anywhere in Europe, start digging for treasure, and probably hit pay dirt. So, we had better get started! One treasure, at least, has slipped through our hands. It has been accounted for and already returned to the owner. Listen to this news clip I found,

> *Treasures stolen from a Russian museum during the Second World War have come home to Momma. Two crates with hundreds of rare exhibits that were stolen in 1941 were returned to Russia by a Wehrmacht doctor's son in an attempt to atone for the sins of his father's generation.*
> *He sent the parcel to a museum in the city of Tver, north of Moscow. The unsuspecting museum employees were stunned when they opened the parcel and found 480 objects, including extremely rare and valuable collections of crosses, archeological findings, and icons.*

"One less treasure to worry about, but that must be the same treasure we had read about earlier. We just didn't know who had returned it," Saul said.

Other Russian treasures were spirited back to Russia after the death of Hitler. In June 1945, three chests holding gold and silver items were seen being loaded onto a Moscow-bound plane.

The gold necklaces and eagle brooches, dating back to the fifth to eighth centuries, once again became visible to the public in a display at Moscow's Pushkin State Museum. What a sight they must be! I managed to compile many fascinating notes on the subject of WWII treasures.

"Hey guys," I said as we sped along toward the Frankfurt airport, "Are we still going to fly into Canada to find the now even more elusive Karl and s-woman, or are we going to seek our fortunes here in Europe? We're already strategically placed to investigate any number of treasure clues."

Just then, before either of my companions could venture an answer, a black Mercedes sped up alongside our little rented Volkswagen. For no apparent reason, it careened right into us.

Wham!

"What was that for?" I yelled, messaging my jarred neck.

Because the windows had darkened glass, it was impossible to see inside the attack vehicle. But it was apparent that the driver had no intention of stopping. In fact s/he was positioning for another collision.

Saul, who was driving, made good use of his soccer-honed quick reflexes. In reaction to the larger car ramming us, he steered the car in the direction the impact sent it, speeding across several lanes and down an exit ramp. He gunned the engine, which seemed to make little difference in the four-cylinder car's speed.

We figured that the other car would have to take the next exit and double back, if he intended to follow. Saul careened onto the next side road we came to.

The rutted dirt and gravel road must at one time have been used for transporting logs from the forest. It was unpaved and deeply rutted. It seemed to have had little use in recent times.

The forest itself, once the victim of logging, had since regained its former density. It soon swallowed our little vehicle from sight.

We had pulled off the side of the road and as far into the woods as possible. Concealing the car with fallen branches and leaves provided a false sense of security.

When convinced that it could no longer be seen, we trudged off through the woods, keeping our path parallel to the rutted and overgrown road. We were hoping to find a cabin or, perhaps, a restaurant (just kidding) where we could seek shelter. Evening would soon be upon us.

Hearing a vehicle approaching from a distance motivated us to pick up our pace. We were hopeful that it was not the car that had pushed us off the road. Just in case, we intended to stay out of sight.

After hiking for close to an hour, we at last saw a break in the trees. A clearing was just ahead.

As we drew closer, we heard voices. Slipping to the edge of the forest, we peered out. We were near a lake. In the background were jagged snow-covered mountains.

The voices we heard belonged to members of what looked like a lake salvage team. There were individuals in scuba gear. Others were manning boats with hydraulic powered pulleys.

As quickly as one boat returned to shore, another went out to the middle of the lake to take its place. Had we stumbled upon a treasure hunt?

It must have been an international team. Several unfamiliar languages were being spoken. There was no cabin, but there was a plethora of trailers that people were constantly entering and existing. One trailer in particular seemed to be heavily guarded.

"Perhaps that's where the salvaged treasures are kept," I mumbled under my breath. "Should we try to talk to someone, or should we try to find our way out of here without being noticed? We have no way of knowing if this group will be friend or foe."

"Let me talk to dem," Arturo said. "I speak several languages, so may seem a little less foreign and threatening."

Saul and I rolled eyes at each other. Arturo was multilingual, but if he spoke every language with the same accent that he spoke English. Well...

After several long moments of conversation with a scuba diver recently returned from the lake, Arturo sauntered back to where Saul and I were still huddled at the edge of the trees. He faced the lake with a nonchalant shrug, should anyone be watching, and said through his heavy Polish accent,

"Dese blokes are a little possessive of de area, but otherwise okay. De lad I was speaking wit said dat dis is just one of several sites in de area dey are checking out."

"Der are tree treasures dey are hoping to find," he continued. "Dey're hoping to discover gold bars in dis lake. Another of de treasures is $500,000,000 worth of stolen artwork, including works from some of my favorite masters, Monet, Manet, Cezanne and master pieces by other artists.

"De rest of the loot includes sculptures, priceless tapestries, paintings and carpets. Dat treasure, according to documents found in the Wehrmacht archives, are tought to be stored in two different subterranean caverns in the Erzebirge Mountains, near the Czeck-German border.

"You said there were three," I reminded him.

"Oh," said Arturo. "Dere are rumors of a Nazi bunker containing de secret gold reserves of de Tird Reich. Digging will soon commence on dat site, which is somewhere in a forest near Leipzig."

Wait, isn't that four?

"They're using old RAF surveillance photographs to help pinpoint de site," Arturo continued. "De Germans bombed dat area in 1944, hoping to conceal de treasure, no doubt."

"We have the scoop on so many treasures here on the continent," I commented. "I think it would be foolhardy to travel to Nova Scotia right now, even if Karl and S-woman, if she's still alive, and I suspect she is, are there." After a moment, I continued, "The treasures you mentioned are thought to be in caverns. What are they hoping to find in this lake?"

Chapter 46

Snuggling in their cozy room in the Swiss hotel, slut-woman and Karl chortled over the façade they had created in Nova Scotia. They were at the hotel decorated with pictures of the devil, no less.

For them, their coup in Nova Scotia was something to celebrate. They felt little remorse about the death of the woman whom they had sprayed with the noxious perfume and then lured into the ravenous coyotes' midst. The only regret that slut-woman had was that the victim had not been Elyse.

A positive ID would be impossible. Authorities had access to sophisticated identification tests. But nothing was left to test. The remains left by the Coywolves had been picked over by vultures. The only evidence that the event even occurred were the eyewitness accounts provided by other hikers in the area.

The Slarls were certain that their ploy would be sufficient to draw Elyse and her companions, as well as others who may be following them, away from the Lünersee to Nova Scotia. Their adversaries would want to verify the tragic and gruesome events.

Such a distraction would allow Karl and Mindy enough time to double back to Austria and search for the stamps, as well as other treasures, unhindered.

In the meantime they decided to get a little R & R. They would kick back, relax and enjoy the ambiance of the devil worshipping hotel.

They might even indulge in a few activities up at the chateaux. This was the very same estate that captivated Elyse's interest when she was last here. Shrouded in mystery, the gloomy structure cast an even gloomier shadow from its perch above the village. Strange events were rumored to take place there.

Chapter 47

"Aha, another treasure, another argument for remaining on this side of the ocean," said I from the back seat. "Have you two ever realized the potential for finding Nazi-looted treasure in Russia and Spain, in addition to Austria and Germany? And if we Americans ever thought that the British were grateful for our participation in the war, listen and learn,"

> *On a cold, shivery February morning in 1945, there was a clandestine meeting among German, British, and Spanish agents. Held in the Center of Madrid in a plush top floor office, the meeting was attended by the Director of a Spanish Institute and heads of the German and British Secret Service.*
> *The topic was "How to divide up the Nazi gold." The British wanted to protect the gold from falling into AMERICAN hands.*
> *The Germans wanted Franco to protect the gold so that it would be available for the post war reconstruction of Germany. According to the diary of the Director of a Spanish institute,*
> *The gold looted by the Nazis should never have been in Spain, nor should it have fallen into the British hands. Not only did the treasure include gold ingots looted from the bank accounts of Jews across Europe, but it also included gold from more sinister sources, like tooth gold from people exterminated in the camps.*

The gold in question had an estimated value of at least 138 million dollars. It had been stored in a series of safe deposit boxes at the institute over the last few years.

In an attempt to recover some of the booty, a few Nazi hunters and a Spanish investigator speculated which of the Nazi hierarchy might have it.

They compiled a suspect list. The list contained the names of ten Nazis living in Spain during the 1990s. When they handed their list of suspects to former PP President Aznar, he insisted that nothing could be done.

Chapter 48

As anxious as I was to head for Lünersee, Arturo and Saul persuaded me to make a wee detour to Spain. This excursion would set us back a couple weeks, but so what.

Maybe we could solve the mystery of the missing gold in Spain. We received a big breakthrough when we stumbled upon the elderly widow of the former director of the Spanish Institute.

Her late husband's diary, to our delight, contained entries for 1945. The entries described a string of meetings in Madrid with both English and German agents.

Most interesting of all was the entry for April 19, 1945. It noted that the gold had been placed on a train bound for Tarifa. From there, it was to be transferred to a building in Gibraltar.

We paid close attention to the Director's wife's narrative. Using snippets from her husband's diary to fill in the blanks, we gleaned that the gold had been stored in strong boxes used to cart it away.

Mrs. *Director* said she had often wondered what had become of her best linens and tablecloths during this period. Passages from the diary cleared up that mystery.

They indicated that the lost items were used to cover the boxes and carts used to transport the gold. The coverings concealed the contents from prying eyes.

Again, having no *formal* schedule to keep, we headed for Gibraltar. There we met with authorities who insisted that there was no gold there.

We spent days of useless pressuring of Gibraltar authorities. When we received no new information, we conceded that that particular gold trail had grown cold, ending in Gibraltar.

We didn't find the gold. What we did come up with was a reasonable explanation of why much of the gold ended in Spain, Gibraltar in particular.

If there were gold in Gibraltar, it was gold that had been stripped from the nations invaded by the Nazis. It was melted into ingots, which were used by the Germans throughout the war and around Europe to purchase raw materials.

Germany bought most of its iron ore from Spain, paying for it with the only method it had—gold. After the war's end in 1945, an audit was performed of captured German *Reichbank* records, statements by Swiss banking officials and other seized records. The audit revealed that during the war, Spain had acquired, in tons of gold the equivalent of approximately 138 million US dollars. Mucho pesetas!

After negotiations, Spain agreed to repatriate a mere 114,000 dollars of gold. When assenting to reimburse this amount, there was another part to the agreement.

The Allies had to issue a statement insisting that Spain was never aware that the gold had been looted by the Nazis in the first place. Spain never showed an interest in locating the many Nazis living there.

Little has changed since the 1970s. The Nazis, warmly received by Franco, still live unprosecuted in Spain. It was only after Nazi hunters tracked down Aribert Heim, *Doctor Death*, that the world became aware of Spain's role in harboring Nazi wealth and Nazis themselves

"Is dis because Spain was in agreement with Germany? So where do dey tink de gold is now?" Arturo asked. "Is der anyting dat provides a clue?"

"Well, some say that it's still in safe deposit boxes in Gibraltar," I answered, "which I very much doubt. More than likely, a lot of the stolen wealth was used to help Germans flee. Some fled to Spain and many fled to South America." I continued, "I'll bet if we did a little sleuthing in Gibraltar, we would encounter some individuals old enough to remember the gold or some who have heard tales about it."

However, with so many other, more glamorous treasures to explore, we decided to head northeast again, on towards our Austrian destination.

Just then, I noticed that Arturo was wearing a beautiful enameled cross.

"Arturo, that cross is exquisite. Where did you get it? I don't remember your wearing before," I exclaimed.

Arturo launched into its provenance, a little too quickly if you ask me. The explanation sounded well-rehearsed.

"It is a replica," he claimed, "It was discovered among odder (other) jewelry in a junk container at an estate sale in Logs, France.

"Before de war, the cross was featured in the collection of a Polish Countess Isabella Dzialynska. With the war impending, some of the gems were buried on the castle grounds where they were found by de Nazis in 1941.

"Three years later, with the tide of war turning, the looted items were moved, on orders from Adolf Hitler, to Castle Fischhorn. From there they were once again pillaged during de chaos surrounding de end of WWII," he continued. "Dis medieval processional cross was rediscovered decades later in an Austrian garbage bin. But before being returned to de heirs of the countess who owned it before the war, it was sketched and replicated."

Arturo swore that the one he wore was a replication. He seemed a tad too defensive in my opinion.

My mind wondered for a moment. *What are we going to do with the stamps—if we ever find them? Could I entrust Saul and Arturo to help turn them over to the heirs of the rightful owner?*

Back to the problem of Arturo's new found jewelry: A little research revealed a statement from the *Commission for Looted Art in Europe,* a London-based organization which helps families recover property stolen by the Nazis.

This statement confirmed that the Limoges enamel cross was part of the collection from the Goluchow Castle in Poland.

I took a closer look at Arturo's *replication.* I could see that the enchanting 13th-century-style cross was adorned with enameled plaques, featuring images of the crucifixion and the apostles.

"Isn't that thing too heavy to wear?" I queried Arturo.

He just shrugged and said, "It's fake, remember. Not heavy at all."

I took another hard look at the cross. It stimulated a memory that was knocking around in the back of my mind, but couldn't quite surface.

Arturo continued to speak,

"I taught that you might be interested in dis old photograph. I found it in de same trash bin as de cross."

Was this yet another clue from another old photograph? I snatched the photograph from Arturo's hands. The picture showed a young soldier posing with his parents. It was typical of the photos that young soldiers took to battle with them to remind themselves of their family.

But this snapshot was unusual in that it had a series of numbers scrawled on its back in faded blue ink. Photographs seemed to be a fertile ground for clues.

Could this one unlock one of the treasure mysteries? Perhaps it held the secret to the whereabouts of a hoard of looted Nazi gold. It was possible, judging from the inscription, that his young soldier served under Rommel. If that were the case, then we may have yet another hot clue to follow.

Rommel is reputed to having hidden gold, but perhaps not for Hitler and the Third Reich. Rommel was one of the plotters implicated in the attempt to assassinate Hitler.

"Aww man," I whined, "How many treasures can we hunt? I vote that, for now, we confine our activities to the European front. Then, if we meet with success, and, only then, will we expand our efforts to other continents and treasures. Our resources are limited, making it necessary to squeeze in a little work now and again."

Saul, who had been an amazingly quiet travel companion on this leg of the trip, agreed.

"Arturo has the magazine, I have the museum, and we both have Interpol cases stacking up on our Internet desks," he continued, "I vote with you, Elyse. We need to create a plan and stick with it. That's not to say that we can't combine some of the treasure explorations with our Interpol cases and expense some of our travel in that manner, eh? But we can't be rushing off in all directions. These treasures have been mysteries for more than 60 years. They'll keep."

So what's a few more months?

Chapter 49

Traveling long distances can be wearisome. I felt the
need to amuse my traveling companions. Car travel was
pretty boring at best. I wanted to keep their minds from
drifting to thoughts of returning to Nova Scotia or work
responsibilities.

I sought to distract them from thoughts of the Slarls and
their shenanigans. I didn't need for them to drool over
Rommel's gold, surreptitiously planning a trip to North
Africa to search for it. So, I began to entertain my two
companions with a ghost story or two.

"Listen to this, guys! See if these ghost stories having
roots in World War II grip your fancy!

> *A ghost, believed to date from the war-plagued 1940s,
> has returned to haunt an old asylum known as
> Vaterholmen. The former asylum is now being used to
> house refugees in the north of Norway.*
>
> *One early January morning in 2010, the police were
> called out to the site by terrified residents. Residents
> gathered outside the building claimed that a ghost that
> had been opening and shutting drawers and closets
> throughout the night.*
>
> *Even the arrival of the police failed to calm the situation.
> Many residents refused to go back inside. When the
> officers searched the building, their investigation failed to
> find the cause of the incidents. After a while, the police
> announced their investigation as closed.*
>
> *The Norwegian media gave the story much publicity. The
> asylum already enjoyed a reputation for being haunted.
> Norway's representative for the Psychical Research
> Foundation, reported the following: that the Vaterholmen
> is haunted is not something new. Rumors that this old
> lieutenant's house is spooked have been floating about for
> years. To substantiate these claims, several people shared
> their experiences. Among them is Anna Kristiansen, once
> a cleaning lady at the building,*
>
> *One time, while she was dusting one of the bedrooms, she
> heard footsteps coming towards her from one of the beds
> and then returning again to the bed. She is still puzzled*

several years later, telling a Norwegian film crew: 'It was like the person was walking on tiptoe.

Anna, who did not believe in ghosts when she started there sure does today.

There is a book devoted to the *Home Guard of Norway* that features the building,

> *Three people from the Home Guard were playing cards when they heard a raucous in the attic. It sounded as if someone was moving furniture around and then walked down the stairs. Who or whatever it was stomped past the room where they had the card game going.*
>
> *One Guard member jumped up and went running out to intercept the suspected intruder to find out what he was doing there and to see if he had taken anything.*
>
> *He got a big surprise when he reached the door. It had been snowing all day, but there were no footprints outside. There were no footprints from anyone coming towards the house or going away; or of anyone who might have been standing there.*
>
> *Perplexed, he went up to fetch his two friends. After looking about, they were as bewildered as he, especially after hearing the footsteps and all the noise in the attic.*

Arturo started to interrupt,

"Vell, vat about going up in de attic. Did dey go up and look around?"

Saul interrupted,

"Isn't that where we were going to stay tonight?"

"Don't know and maybe not," I said, responding to both their questions.

"There is some speculation as to the identity of the ghost. So, if we do stay there, at least we'll know who we're up against."

But, wait! The story didn't end there,

> *During World War II, the house was occupied by German troops. One young soldier named Josef received orders sending him to the Eastern Front, from where he had just returned.*

Karl Johansen, a local man, remembers Josef very well. He recalls him crying when he received his orders. So depressed by the news and unable to face the prospect of returning to the front again, Josef hanged himself in one of the rooms. Ever since then, although some people have had peaceful nights there, a multitude of others, in fact most, have reported unnerving experiences that they believe is the restless spirit of Josef.

War is horrendous, destroying life and property. As such, it generates more ghost stories than other activities, something few may realize.

Not many of the tales surfacing from war eras rival the tale of the crew members of three WWII Douglas DB-7 Boston bombers. As the story goes, these men (or ghosts) completed and signed their debriefing reports after they'd been shot down and killed.

I preceded this tale with some spooky background music downloaded at our last wireless site. I then shared the tale in a hushed, somber voice,

After the fall of France, a squadron of British Bostons prepared for a strike at German coastal defenses. At the bomber base, an RAF air marshal was present to oversee the attack and secure vital intelligence on enemy positions from returning crews.

The air marshal waited, carefully calculating when the aircraft would be due back. At the hour he expected their return, he heard the sound of three, possibly four, sets of American-built engines approaching.

He heard the aircraft land. He heard their engines shut down. He heard vehicles driving up to the operations building, the opening and closing of doors and the sound of booted footsteps.

Finally, the crew of three Bostons stood before the air marshal, their faces expressionless masks, concealing the terror of what they had just been through.

Not wishing to waste any time, the air marshal advised the crew to fill out their debriefing reports, making certain that they included their names, rank, serial numbers, time and date, and signature. He then recommended to them to go and have a well-deserved

drink. The men completed the task as bade, and then filed
from the room, silent the entire time.
When the air marshal's aide entered shortly afterward,
he shared the horrific news that the men had all been
killed. He had a great deal of trouble convincing the
officer that the entire squadron had been shot down over
their targets.

Intelligence confirmed the tragedy, but the air marshal perplexed the aide and intelligence officers further when he waved at them the written and signed reports from the three crew members. Later, it was confirmed that everyone on the mission had been killed. No prisoners were taken; there were no survivors.

What's particularly remarkable about this case is the written evidence provided by the completed forms. The explanation provided? People who die suddenly and violently commonly appear to the living. Often they appear to loved ones or people who are expecting them.

Huh?

Some *research* suggests this is due to the dead not realizing they are dead. They continue as though still alive. But when spirits find they have no impact on the world, that they are unable to write or communicate, they usually begin to understand they have passed on.

This case is exceptional in that the spirits maintained the ability to communicate and to write. Death, it seems, held no such disadvantages for these incredible men. They were determined to complete their mission – and sign off on the paperwork to make it official.

Which is more bizarre, the episode or the explanation?
It's a tossup in my opinion.

Arturo, always prone to being a little superstitious, had become a shade paler during the tale.

Chapter 50

I had one more touching story of the ghostly genre that I wanted to share with my partners.

Klyzma is one of the dozens of tiny Russian villages making up the region is known as Podmoskovi. An ancient place, dating to the middle of the 15th century, it has in recent years become, like all of the surrounding towns and villages, *a bedroom community* for the capitol.

Klyzma is populated by mid and upper level business people and civil servants who don't mind the twenty minute commute (I would kill to have a twenty minute commute) into Moscow, in exchange for peace and quiet and good air. These *new* people reside side by side with families who have lived in the area for generations, some for centuries.

In the mid-forties, a period which many people refer to as the 'late unpleasantness,' the region had other guests, who were not quite as welcome.

The little town was part and parcel of a strip of land that changed hands between the Wehrmacht and the Red Army on a weekly, sometimes hourly basis. Where in lay its value? The little town sits at a natural ford on the Ucha River. Its geographical value lay in the fact that at this point the river was shallow enough to cross without a bridge. Warring armies could cross here with ease.

Like most of the other villages in this area, Klyzma has one more-or-less paved main street, a half a dozen tiny shops and kiosks, and about as many houses.

There is a school that was built around the turn of the twentieth century. There are five or six apartment buildings constructed in the late forties and early fifties.

Then there is a cemetery, sitting off by itself on the western fringe of the village and surrounded by fir trees. It is connected to the town by a narrow, winding, one lane dirt road that leads to the village church.

Every day, late in the afternoon, about sundown, when passing the cemetery, you will see a very elderly couple with a small girl standing in the cemetery. The old couple, no doubt in their nineties, tends a tiny grave surrounded by a wrought iron fence. All the while, a little girl silently plays in the snow or in the dirt, depending on the season.

The routine is repeated every day without fail, rain or shine. The old man and old woman appear to be in their late seventies. The little girl looks to be about six or seven. On closer scrutiny, you will see that the man's left hand is stiff, and motionless, encased in single, black leather glove. The old woman helps him to lift things that he can't manage with his artificial limb. A touching sight it is.

The grave they tend has a simple monument. Unlike the others in the area, there is no likeness of the deceased attached to it. Instead, it bears the simple inscription: *Cherkirova, Valeriya Borisovna, 18 April, 1935 - 25 June, 1941.*

Beneath this is the simple inscription, "Our Little Heroine." Around the stone is attached a tattered red ribbon, from which hangs the solid gold star of the Order of Hero of the Soviet Union.

The medal does not belong to little *Valeriya*, although it should. It was, instead, presented to her father, the former foreman of the Klyzma Tractor Factory during wartime.

His missing left hand, lost in a factory accident, prevented him from serving in the red army when the Germans invaded Russia in May of 1941. Instead, he and his wife, who also worked in the factory, stayed at their posts. They worked side by side with others who were too old, too young or too lame, and kept the factory going. They produced tank motors instead of tractors.

The villagers who share the story do so with great emotional difficulty,

> *Little Valeriya was gathering berries on the outskirts of the village one late June afternoon when she heard a strange sound. It sounded like the tractors that her daddy's factory made, only lots of them... dozens, maybe even hundreds.*
> *She climbed up on a small hill to take a better look and was amazed at what she saw in the far distance. She had never seen so many tractors before. What she saw were, tanks, many, many tanks.*

This was the first advance of the mighty German juggernaut. Having crossed the shallow waters of the Ucha River at the ford, they were advancing toward Klyzma as part of the German attempt to encircle Moscow.

Despite being just a tiny child, Valeriya was aware that her country was at war. She could tell that these tanks did not look like the ones her Daddy's factory made. They had black crosses on them like the ones her Daddy told her the Germans used on their tanks.

Valeriya was desperate to warn someone. She remembered what she must do. Her daddy had told her. She had to let the village know that those tanks were coming.

Like all villages in the area, Klyzma had an old, hand-cranked siren that was mounted on a short platform. This siren, most often used to summon the fire brigade when there was a blaze could be heard all over the surrounding area. It was never, never used except in an emergency.

Valeriya ran as fast as her little legs would carry her to the center of the village where the platform was. She scampered up the steps and grabbed hold of the crank. She tried to swing it down. It was old and rusty and slow to respond.

The crank handle was above her head. She jumped to reach it. It took all of her weight to get it to move at all. At first it moved slowly.

She hung there, in the air, her tiny feet not quite touching the ground. It began to move, and, then, under the weight of her little body, it began to creak and groan and then to swing.

The siren began to sound its low, mournful cry. In the factory, on the other side of the village, Valeriya's mother and father, and the rest of the workers dropped everything when they heard the sound and ran outside to investigate.

Once out of the factory, there was no mistaking the rumble of the tank motors. Boris and most of the workers ran to get the weapons that the Government had left for them for just such an emergency. Valeriya's mother cranked at the single telephone in the factory to summon help.

The first 75mm German shell exploded the signal tower just as factory men came into view. The workers had no idea who was giving off the alarm. They never found a body.

The villagers, grim and determined, dug in and fought off the Germans until the Red Air Force came to the rescue. Since it was only one company of the German army, they were able to hold on to their village.

In the confusion, no one thought to look for little Valeriya. It was assumed that she had hidden somewhere as she had been taught to do. She would come home as soon as she saw that it was safe.

It was not until the next day that they discovered who had saved the village by sounding the alert. In the ashes and rubble of the crater that had once been the signal tower, a stunned father found his little girl's pail and one of her tiny shoes.

Boris Cherkirov won the Order of Hero of the Soviet Union that day, for his part in leading his factory workers in their dogged defense of Klyzma. After the war was over, he quietly hung the medal around his only child's headstone.

As many can attest to, the old couple tends the grave as the little girl who is with them plays at their feet. As they leave the graveyard, little Valeriya waves goodbye to them. She then fades into the mist that forms around her tiny grave.

The Cherkirov's can't see her, so they don't know she's there, but everyone else can see her.

There was not a dry eye when the story was finished.

"Well guys, where do you want to sleep tonight?"

Chapter 51

We had rolled our way back from Spain to Austria. At a local Austrian pub where we stopped for refreshment, I happened into some WWII veterans who were only too eager to share their war memories of *real* ghosts—as Patton's Ghost Troops were referred to.

As we consumed brats and beer, Henry Ritter, a 92 year old World War II veteran shared memories of his time in the U.S. Army during World War II with Company C, 22nd Armored Engineers, 5th Armored Division. This division saw some of the worst fighting of the war. According to Harry,

> We were with Patton's Third Army, the unit referred to as Patton's Ghost Troops, because they never knew where we were, or where we would be next. We didn't realize we had that distinction until the war was almost over.
>
> It was the *Battle of Hürtgen Forest*, a series of fierce battles between American and German troops from Sept. 19, 1944, to February 10, 1945. The battle took place in an area just east of the German-Belgian border. We had five campaign stars for the division—all individual battles—and we were the only engineer outfit decorated with a Presidential Citation. The division also received the French medal, the *Croix de Guerre* with the Silver Star.
>
> Those five battles included the *Battle of the Bulge*, known by the Germans as the Ardennes Offensive. The worst were the two forest battles.
>
> Forests weren't made for armored divisions. They provide no room to maneuver and you're lucky to have one little dirt road for access.
>
> The troops took a beating, because as soon as they access a side road, they got pushed off. The enemy had all access points covered. We lost a lot of men. We went in with 15 tanks and came out with just three.
>
> After the company finished with the *Battle of Hürtgen Forest*, they were committed to the *Battle of the Bulge*, which was just beginning,
>
> It was a busy time for them. They had to clear the mines and build bridges. If a river or a stream were impassable, we put up a bridge. When mine fields posed a hazard, they

had to go in there and clean out the mine fields. They would be in there cleaning the mine fields while the enemy was shelling them.

Kind of scary, huh? The old guy shared some humorous stories as well. His memory was darn sharp for someone in his nineties,

> Although our outfit had its share of casualties, no matter what the crisis, there was always something or someone to relieve the tension. My driver, nicknamed Junebug, was a real character. He provided enough humor for everyone. One day when we were taking sporadic fire, we happened upon a stray police dog. Now this dog was able to sense before any of us when an artillery shell was headed our way. I guess it was his keen sense of hearing.
> The dog would race and always beat Junebug to his foxhole and jump in before Junebug could. When Junebug arrived, huffing and puffing, he would jump into the foxhole, pick up the dog and then throw him out, but the dog would jump right back in. These antics provided hysterical comic relief for half the outfit. They would sit there, laughing hysterically while watching Junebug fighting the dog for his spot.

He continued with his ruminations,

> The days were long and hard with few breaks and little sleep. One of the toughest things about our existence was the hours that we put in on the roads.
> Rising early, we would eat cold eggs from a can and hit the road by dawn. We ate K-rations on the go, often traveling until after midnight, eat more K-rations, and then grab a quick nap. We got so used to drinking lukewarm coffee with no milk or sugar that I still drink that way even now.

"Saul must be a relative of yours," I chuckled, because that was the way Saul drank his coffee as well.

Having had a hearty lunch and access to a few great stories, we took our leave. Once in the car, Arturo launched into a narrative about the latest news on the treasure hunting front,

"When we were back at de lake, I heard Christian Handutch speaking to a CNN reporter. He said dat Heinz-Peter Hirschi, who had been paying for de excavation, told him to leave, to get out right away.

"Hirschi wants to make de expedition more credible by being surrounded by scientists rather den fortune hunters. Handutch also said he never believed in the Amber Room theory. He said that he never talked about finding de Amber Room anywhere around here. Dat was all Hirschi's idea."

"Hmm! Why are you so indignant about this, Arturo? Is he a friend of yours?" I asked.

"Well, yeah, in a way," Arturo said. "I've interviewed him for articles before. I like de guy, and it just seems like a bad way to conduct business. Dis will come back to bite Hirschi. Mark my words."

"Will do." With that said, I shared another *real life* ghost story.

It seemed that Rommel also had ghost troops.

> *Erwin Rommel's 7 Panzer-Division, was later nicknamed Gespenster-Division, or the 'Ghost Division.' The speed and surprise it was consistently able to achieve often confused even the German High Command with its whereabouts. Its collective stamina was nothing to sneeze at either. The 7-Panzer-Division set the record for the longest thrust by tanks in one day. They covered nearly 320 kilometers (200 mi).*
>
> *While many were impressed with the division's speed and success, there were just as many who, perhaps because of envy, decried Rommel's tactics, saying that they were foolhardy.*
>
> *They claimed that he took too many risks, showing a lack of experience and an underdeveloped sense of judgment.*
>
> *Others complained because he did not acknowledge their contributions to his victories. No doubt, these grumblings were rooted in jealousy.*

Chapter 52

There were many fascinating tidbits about the war and the treasures stolen during the war. Deviating a little from talk of treasure, I continued entertaining Saul and Arturo with fascinating WWII stories as we drove,

> In June 1944, a secret U.S. Army unit went into action in Normandy. The weapons they deployed were decidedly unusual: hundreds of inflatable tanks and a one-of-a-kind collection of sound effects records. Their mission was to bluff, deceive, and use trickery to save lives.
> Many involved with creating the illusion were artists. Some would become famous later, including a budding fashion designer named Bill Blass. These talented individuals painted and sketched their way across Europe, creating a unique visual record of their journey.
> Their war efforts reached a pinnacle in Normandy. The story of what these men accomplished in Normandy was hushed up by the Pentagon for more than forty years.
> Why? Their heroism should have been commemorated with a stamp!

****

These remarkable artists helped create the charade of the presence of a large, well-equipped military endeavor. They were led by non-other than the fierce war hero, Patton, who, under a cloak of great secrecy, had been brought to England from Sicily,

> First, General Eisenhower, Supreme Commander of the Allied forces, assigned to Patton two jobs. Patton was to command the Third Army, making it ready for deployment in France after the invasion.
> In addition, Eisenhower gave General Patton command of the First United States Army Group (FUSAG). He was to head Operation Quicksilver, using the fictitious army created to fool the Germans. It was essential that both assignments be kept secret.

The artists created dummy tanks, artillery pieces, trucks, jeeps and planes and even dummy ships. In the meantime, Patton got the Third Army, a force of over 250,000 men ready for combat. When Patton finally did land in France, the army kept his arrival under wraps so that Operation Quicksilver could continue to fool the Germans.

On June 6 1944, no doubt feeling a little foolish, Patton was sitting on the shores of England, as the head of the fake army. With weapons and tanks made from rubber and painted cardboard, he was part of the largest and most successful deception operation of World War II.

Operation Quicksilver was part of a larger deception plan called *Operation Fortitude South/Operation Bodyguard. The plan was used to cloak the buildup of the Allied Army and to disguise the destination of the invasion.*

Few battles of World War II are as enduring in the American public consciousness as the Allied invasion of Normandy on June 6, 1944. This assault, an event known to most people as D-Day, was the largest amphibious landing in military history. It was of paramount importance to the Allies.

If this mission were successful, it meant that France, which had been in Germany's grip for four long years, would be liberated. This setup would provide the Allies' best chance for pushing Hitler's weakened army back to Berlin.

Much was at stake. Failure of the mission meant that Germany would have another year to bolster its faltering army. In that scenario, they would gain new impetus for defeating the soviet offensive on the eastern front.

They would have time to fully develop new intercontinental aircraft and new weapons in the form of powerful rockets, more powerful than the intercontinental ballistic missiles that existed at that time.

Chapter 53

In 1943, the Allies had decided to invade in Normandy. It was within fighter cover of British airfields and was considered a less likely site than Calais, a town and major ferry point in northern France.

The intent was to confuse the Germans about the actual invasions site and lead them to believe that Calais was the intended target. So, elaborate plans were enacted to make them think Calais was the true target.

This was where the fake army led by General Patton came into play. To further enhance the subterfuge, a fleet of unseaworthy landing craft was placed in British ports across from Calais.

The icing on the cake for the hoax was the much publicized appointment of General George Patton as commander of the First U.S. Army Group.

German leaders were convinced. They were so persuaded that they kept the Fifteenth Army in the Calais area, thinking that this was to be the site of the Allied invasion.

How best to determine when this amphibious invasion would occur? Several factors influenced the setting of the date.

Influencing factors included the tides, which needed to be low when the invasion force struck. The weather, which required minimal winds to reduce choppy seas, was another factor.

Last, but not least, was the lighting. The invasion required moonlight in the evening and enough early morning sunlight at the moment the assault was to begin.

The date and time of the invasion, based on such factors, were determined to be best executed anytime from early May to early June. June 5 became the pre-determined date.

Unfortunately, bad weather forced Eisenhower to postpone the event for another 24 hours. The decision to delay was difficult.

If the Germans caught on, even at the last minute, they could bolster defenses at the invasion point. So, even though the weather report for June 6 wasn't perfect, Eisenhower opposed postponing the invasion again.

The assembled invasion force consisted of more than 1.5 million troops. Accompanying the fleet were 11,000 fighter planes, bombers, transport planes, and gliders.

An estimated 60 German divisions were on the other side. It was a formidable defense, and many in the German High Command thought it was invincible. But the allied air, land and sea attack was so well-coordinated that the Germans' initial reaction was one of utter chaos.

The Germans were caught flat-footed. Many of the German field commanders were missing. Field Marshal Erwin Rommel, overall commander of German troops in the area, had returned home to Germany for his wife's birthday party. He had left his chief of staff to oversee Army Group B.

Another general, the commander of the Seventh Army, was also away from headquarters, attending a practice war game in Rennes. The commander of the I SS Panzer Corps, and was in Brussels on a shopping trip with his mistress.

Even though the invasion resulted in ferocious fighting and grave loss of life, it was apparent that the allied charade had worked! The Allies had succeeded in gaining a foothold on the French coast. They were poised to liberate the country and push on toward Berlin.

Contributing to the allied success was Hitler himself. Hitler became his commanders' worst enemy. He seized control from them and attempted to direct the German defense from his command post some 600 miles away.

In mid-June he added an additional Panzer division to the two already being sent to reinforce the Normandy defense to begin a massive counteroffensive.

He ordered all troops to hold their present positions, overriding Rommel and Rundstedst's insistence that any divisions sent to Normandy would arrive late with insufficient supplies. They would likely be eliminated by Allied firepower.

Chapter 54

As significant as the invasion of Normandy was, I thought that I would easily find many stamps commemorating the event. After all, it changed the course of the war and an estimated 15,000 Allied soldiers were killed or wounded during the first day alone.

German losses were approximately the same. According to a report by Field Marshal Erwin Rommel, an instrumental part of the German defense command, his casualties for that month were 28 generals, 354 commanders, and approximately 250,000 men.

Besides the loss of human life, the invasion prevented the Germans from experiencing success along the Russian front. Nor were they able to continue the development of long-range missiles and aircraft.

So, wouldn't it be a natural assumption that the government would later issue a series of stamps to commemorate this historic event? Germany may not have chosen to do so, but certainly for the participating allies, the U.S., England, and the French resistant fighters would.

Wouldn't they?

There is evidence that other stamps were issued in memory of the war's activities and its martyrs. Russia issued five postage stamps marking the 55th anniversary of the end of World War II.

Japan issued four postage stamps with World War II related themes, part of a series on the Millennium.

Norfolk Island issued a 75-cent postage stamp showing a list of war dead from World War II.

Guernsey issued six postage stamps marking the 60th anniversary of the Battle of Britain.

****

So, where was the US stamp honoring the action at Normandy? After launching several searches to no avail, at last I did a query for stamps commemorating "invasions." And there it was! It is not flamboyant, but, instead, is a subdued gray and white stamp. Perhaps its somber design is a tribute to the lives lost there.

The stamp displays a map of the French coast ranging from the actual Normandy invasion zone to the imaginary Calais strike point opposite Patton's flimflam. Because this area was coincidental with the Operation Crossbow missions flown from England to counteract the flying bomb and V2 rocket sites assembled by Hitler, the stamp was entitled Operation Crossbow/Normandy Invasion.

Interestingly, the borderlines drawn to highlight the exact geography form a sketch of a crossbow, albeit ready to fire its stealthy and deadly arrow in the opposite direction than history requires.

Perhaps the bland gray and white coloring of the stamp commemorates the secrecy on which the success of the event depended. The current value of this significant stamp appears to be $22.95.

Shouldn't this particular stamp be in hot demand by philatelists who are also World War II enthusiasts? I decided that this would be my first significant purchase. And it is *affordable!*

It then occurred to me that I already had this collector stamp in my possession. It was the stamp on the mystery envelope: *Addressee Unknown: Return to Sender.*

Chapter 55

In awe of the events at Normandy, exhausted and daunted by the prospect of meandering from one treasure site to another, I said,

"Hey, Saul and Arturo, what say you that we just focus on the stamps and put an end to all these shenanigans with slut-woman and Karl? Why are we always on the defensive? For once, why don't we go on the offensive? Instead of reacting to or trying to figure out their next move, let's become more proactive. This may seem silly to you, but I propose that we create a strategy similar to the Invasion of Normandy. We'll create a charade similar to Patton's fake army and armament."

"Um, what do you mean?" Saul asked, rather tentatively. The term "invasion" seemed to have set him on edge.

"The other alternative is to kidnap and then torture them—you know, like popping our gum or eating Doritos for hours on end, until they spill the beans about the treasures. I've had it with all their stupid charades, pretending that one—no, two—no, none, has been killed."

I continued,

"Let's put an end to this farce once and for all. That way, if you two want to treasure hunt, we can spend time going after something we know for sure exists. They've faked their deaths so many times, no one will even be aware that they're missing, or much less care. We don't even know for certain that the stamps still exist. They could have dug them up and distributed or sold the stamps years ago. This could just be a perverted game to them."

We were all in agreement that the stamp farce being played by Karl and slut-woman must end. We needed to find the stamps, or verify, once and for all, that they are gone. That they have either been destroyed or broken up and sold off.

We set about devising a plan. My next suggestion was that we establish a safe house. We then lure in the Slarls by plastering signs with arrows to the safe house. We would promote something they would be unable to resist—*free beer*.

Saul chuckled,

"Well that would certainly draw them in. They and about 1,000,000 thirsty others would be clambering at the door. What we need to do is to separate them, and then convince each one that we have done away with the other. That way they'll become despondent, lose all hope, and confess."

Arturo, a little reticent on the subject, until now, spoke up,

"You mean kidnap dem separately? Dat's a lot of work! And den where do we keep dem and what do we do wid dem after we kidnap dem? Dey would press charges. And Saul and I can't afford a scandal with our Interpol Agent status."

So I chimed in,

"Then we kill them."

I was teasing, of course, but Arturo looked as though he were about to pass out.

"I'm just kidding, Arturo. I can't believe you two are actual Interpol agents. Your schemes are more harebrained than any of mine."

I then seized upon my former inspiration,

"If the troops in the 1940s could pull off a complex charade like Normandy, what's to stop us from creating a similar pretense? If such a plan could fool Hitler and all his generals, then why wouldn't a similar, more up-to-date plan fool the Slarls?

"We could stage broken or cheap equipment at an alternate lake site. We could then hire divers and local villagers to mill about that site.

"We would plant rumors about the existence of treasures of unbelievable value and beauty about to be recovered there. We need a site with a location far enough away from Lünersee to make it inconvenient to shuttle back and forth.

"But we don't want it to be too far. We may need our *Nameless* allies' assistance from time-to-time with the

Slarls, greedy charlatans that they are, and whomever else they've recruited."

I continued most adamantly,

"I forgot to tell you, but I overheard the Slarls discussing a contract with an assassin, a hit man, a killing machine, a wet work specialist ..."

"Okay, okay, we get de point," Arturo interrupted.

Ignoring Arturo's interruption, I continued,

"... could be here in Austria even as we speak, waiting for our search operations to begin. Then he or she could find any number of subtle ways to eliminate me."

Saul, looking startled asked,

"Why didn't you mention this earlier? We definitely need to deflect attention from us. We need to find a villager who resembles you."

Karl and I both interrupted at that juncture, saying in unison,

"But wouldn't it be awful if she were killed as the result of mistaken identity."

Saul, also irritated at being interrupted, continued,

"We need to find a look-alike who could take care of herself and the assassin. She could seduce him, and, perhaps, in a moment of weakness, he would reveal some important detail regarding the plot. Maybe one of the *Nameless* recruits would have an idea of who to recruit. They have so many connections. There's probably a former intelligence person from some country or other just spoiling for a little action."

I had been mulling the plan over in my mind ever since reading about the invasion at Normandy. First, we establish a camp. Then we create a flurry of activity at whatever site we choose.

It would be only a matter of time before the Slarls, and perhaps the assassin, showed up. Maybe they would hang around, curious to find out what was going on.

They would, no doubt, hold back until they thought we were on the very brink of recovering some fabled treasure— perhaps the Amber Room. While they're absorbed with those activities, we should be able to discreetly explore the Lünersee region.

I commented that,

"Our divers could surface periodically with small, enticing clues to convince everyone that both the Amber room and other treasures were buried at the alternative site. After dragging out the scenario, a few skilled *Nameless* members could stage a diving expedition, hauling up crates containing a few artifacts."

They would have to be conspicuous and flamboyant enough to receive local news coverage.

Chapter 56

While everyone focused on the new *find* site, we three, Arturo, Saul, and I, could continue to explore, uninhibited, the shores and depths of Lünersee. We would work during the night or in the early morning hours when there would be less likelihood of surveillance.

I shared the rest of my brilliant plan with the others. It was met with rolling eyes and a few unflattering comments.

"Wait," I said. "I know it can work."

Ignoring the silent jeers, I continued,

"If such a ploy were successful for Patton, then why can't it be for us? His false army charade at Normandy confused the Germans. Why can't we create a similar hoax, pretending to dive and dig at a lake other than, but close to Lünersee? What about Lake Whalen. It's only about a 45 minute drive from here. We could delude all those following us, including the Slarls, long enough to explore the lake shores and the lake itself."

Making the plan feasible, we had our own hi-tech equipment, including sonar, unmanned submarines equipped with cameras, and electro-magnetrons that I *borrowed* at the Lake Toplitz site.

"Well," said Saul,

"Who's going to assist us in our little charade at Lake Whalen?"

I explained that most of the equipment used there could be props—further adopting Patton's deceptive methods. The diving platform in the middle of the lake could be inflatable.

I would call upon some of my *Nameless* contacts because they were good divers and would provide the illusion of credibility to the site. They could actually do a little diving and exploring. It would be a mini vacation for them since they enjoy those activities.

I recruited our faux assistants for the faux cite with their faux equipment, requesting each to bring a complete wet suit, some digging tools, and a tent.

We could also set up a shortwave radio, a CD player, propane stoves along with a stock pile of fragrant foods. We would use walkie-talkies to maintain close contact with them. The goal was to attract as much attention as possible to their site while we maintained a low profile at ours.

In the meantime, the three of us would explore the Lünersee shores, determining where the treasure might be buried. It's supposed to be near a stream located between the lake and cabin.

I just hoped the area wasn't covered by three feet of snow. If that's the case, we'll pitch our tent over the excavation site to obscure our activities.

My expectations were that the Slarls, their allies, and whoever else might be following us, will gravitate to the faux site. This would provide plenty of breathing room and the necessary privacy to explore. The walkie-talkies could provide the connection to our *Nameless* buddies at the faux site.

We began accumulating the gear for both sites, renting the necessary boats, diving equipment, and tents. There would be tents for both lakes, and sleeping bags and diving gear for us.

The Norwegian *Nameless* team had their own equipment, no doubt far superior to those we could provide for them. Any excess equipment could be used for the villagers we would recruit to work along with them.

After a bit of research, the decoy site we settled upon was Lake Whalen, one of the larger lakes in Switzerland. It is also known as Lake *Whalenstadt*, after Whalenstadt Village. Other towns and villages near the lake include Weesen, Quinten, Quarten, and Murg.

The fact that the lake Whalen was only about 32 km away was convenient. It was close enough to be accessible to us and far enough to discourage any shuttling back and forth among spectators who might gather (the Slarls) to watch.

To provide a little geographical and historical information about the area, the Churfirsten mountain range rises steeply on the North side from the lake's level at 419 m to 2,300 m above sea level. The three main rivers feeding into this lake are the *Seez*, *Murgbach*, and *Linth*. The latter continues its course from Whalen to Lake Zurich.

The beauty of the area and the lake in particular provided Hungarian romantic composer Franz Litz the inspiration to compose a solo piano piece called *Au lac de Wallenstadt*. The piece is part of a collection of piano works motivated by the composer's travels in Switzerland during 1830.

Not to dispel any romantic moods, but, we could sink decoy boxes at our new destination so that there would actually be something for the *Nameless* team to haul out. The locals we would hire would, from a distance, have to pass as Saul, Arturo, and me exploring the murky depths, hoping to make incredible discoveries.

At this time, Saul reminded us of something we had overlooked. Some of these Alpine lakes, Lake Toplitz, for example, were so deep that they sustained only life that could survive without oxygen. Some of the most virulent bacteria are anaerobic bacteria. That is, they can survive without oxygen.

Such bacteria secrete toxins that can be destroyed only with great difficulty. They must be subjected to intense heat and high pressure.

This combination of conditions allows steam to reach temperatures far above boiling, destroying the microbes and breaking down some toxins.

There is no escape, and their evil, tiny lives are cut short before they can continue their reign of destruction in another host. Many of these same bacteria are resistant to commonly used antibiotics as well.

****

Perhaps it was now time to call upon Froggy to earn his keep. It was time for us to utilize the little beastie's subcutaneous peptides as antibiotics.

We would administer the antibiotic secretion to ourselves before diving into any oxygen-less water. These were waters where anaerobic bacteria thrived, along with the anaerobic worm. Eww!

We had no conclusive proof that these peptides would protect us from the microbes and the toxins they might secrete. Their use would at least bolster our confidence.

But how were we to administer these untried and untested peptides to ourselves? Should we attempt to harvest an adequate amount—with no harm coming to Froggy? I had developed quite an infection... I mean, affection for the little guy.

Once we had harvested an adequate supply of peptides, we had to decide how to most effectively administer it to ourselves. Should we ingest, inject or use the peptides topically? I turned to look at Saul, who shrugged in response.

"You mean, you don't know?" I screeched.

Saul shrugged again, saying,

"We have two alternatives. We can either apply the antibiotic to ourselves using all three of the available methods of administration, or we can create our own study to see which method of application is most effective. I could use one method, you one, and Arturo another. And then see who survives."

He grinned mischievously.

I queried, unamused.

"Can we harvest a large enough amount to utilize the first option, or even the second option for that matter?"

Saul winked,

"I've been feeding the little fellow extra well. He, in turn, has produced enough peptides for us to apply it to ourselves in a variety of ways for at least a couple weeks. It doesn't require a large amount to be effective."

Chapter 57

Activity commenced at Lake Whalen, the alternative site. The lake we had chosen for this purpose was only about 50 miles from Lake Lünersee and was very similar in terrain. I had already contacted a few of the less nerdy and more physical members of *Nameless*.

Nameless is a spinoff of *Anonymous*, the infamous Internet hacker organization sworn to expose the secret, harmful activities of governments and political figures. They accomplish their exposés with public postings of mysteriously acquired *classified* documents.

Nameless, although they operate at a similar skill level, is less altruistic and much more mercenary than *Anonymous*. They share information but only at great financial cost to the recipient. *Nameless* is also capable of presenting an imposing physical presence when required by specific situations.

As the result of many discussions, a little planning and much persuasion, my cooperative contacts were conducting a dual frontal attack at the excavation site.

After reconnoitering the depths of the lake, they had decided that an above ground exploration would attract more attention. With attention focused on them, we would be better able to skulk about Lake Lünersee.

The plan worked too well. Their activities were so flamboyant, that we, Saul, Arturo, and I, were drawn to the lake to witness the exciting activities. We mingled with the many excited locals and tourists.

The activities also attracted some unsavory, tough-looking individuals. Their bald pates glistened in the sun while Hitler-esque moustaches crawled above their lips.

Each of these characters sported a Swastika-like earing. It resided either in the left ear or protruding from the left cheek.

Ouch!

These individuals observed the proceedings with an intensity that gave me the shivers.

We watched. Our *Nameless* group drilled. Each time the huge drills penetrated the ground, puffs of white dust were thrown into the air, causing spectators in the frontline to cough and retreat a bit. They would brush the powder from their clothing and then return to the scene where the process would repeat itself.

So fascinating were the proceedings, that I found it difficult to contain my own feelings of excitement. Swept up in the moment, I had forgotten that this was a *ruse* site.

Herr Herzog, the mayor of this tiny village, had staked his reputation on the claim that 20m below ground lay crates containing the long-lost Amber Room. If not the Eighth Wonder of the World, as it was sometimes referred to, at the very least, there would be gold and jewels.

He had long dreamed that the fabled, long sought-after intricate chamber of honey, linseed and cognac-infused amber panels, would be discovered in his tiny village. He prayed that it was the Amber Room that they would find.

Herzog shared with the local newspaper,

> People may laugh at me, but I tell you, it took Columbus a long time to be taken seriously enough to be given a new ship to head to the new world.

What provided such conviction to this 53-year old MP for the social democrats in the Swiss assembly? This was a man who had once been focused on the reform of the country's accident insurance laws, not treasure hunts.

What made him think that he may have the key to unlock one of the most tantalizing mysteries of the war—the whereabouts of the Amber Room?

Chapter 58

Two months prior to initiating the "treasure expedition" at Lake Whalen we were approached by a part-time treasure hunter, Christian Handutsch. His real name is concealed at his request, but he and Arturo had once been close.

Christian had some revealing documents in his possession. Desirous of remaining disassociated from any treasure discoveries, he turned the documents over to us. Because of his previous associations with Arturo, he entrusted us to do the right thing with the knowledge contained in the documents,

> My grandfather spoke reluctantly about his involvement in the operation and what he did in the war. If you make it to the site, take a metal detector with you. I dangled mine over the entrance to a cavern, and at once it registered red and orange, an indication of the presence of precious metals.
>
> I inherited his papers when he died, but am now in such poor health that I cannot take up the quest myself. I wish to rely upon altruistic seekers, such as you three, to take up my quest.

Local historical reports support the documentation, describing how, as part of *Operation Sundown*, German military convoys delivered heavy sealed caskets. They hid them in a network of copper and silver mines in the Ore Mountains on the Czech-German border on April 9 1945, in the final weeks of the war.

Unbeknownst to the mayor, we had altered the coordinates a teeny bit before turning them over to him. They now reflected the site as being Lake Whalen. Later, we would explore the Ore mountain site designated by the real coordinates.

We turned over the faked documents to Mayor Herzog. The documents gave new impetus to the search. We created this charade to conceal our own activities over at Lake Lünersee. Of course we felt guilty for the chicanery, but knew that the town would receive unexpected revenue from the tourists drawn in to watch the excavation proceedings. It was a win, win.

Should we succeed in finding the treasures using the unaltered coordinates later on, what then? We had predetermined that we would share the resulting wealth with the mayor and his little town. We would ensure that the noble desire for a new school would become a reality.

What a sensation it would be if fragments or other evidence leading to the remains of the Amber Room were to be discovered near this impoverished little village located in the eastern part of Germany.

Such a find would represent quite a windfall for the downtrodden area, and for us, since amber at this time is at least 12 times more valuable than gold. And the tourist trade for this area would increase more than a hundred fold!

We hung on to the original notebooks and maps Mr. Handutsch found amid the possessions of his late father, Johann. After all, he was a former signaler with the Luftwaffe. He was convinced that the documents pinpointed the precise location of the much sought-after treasure.

Mr. Handutsch's ancient aunt was at the faux excavation site. She focused on the scene with an intensity that belied her years. Having sidled up to her as I drifted through the crowd of onlookers, I heard her sigh as she watched the proceedings.

No doubt, memories had come flooding back. Or, perhaps, she alone was aware that the real clues indicated another site.

The mayoral oratory took off,

"This is an historical moment. We're watching history unfold. I stake my reputation on the claim that only 20m below ground are the crates containing the fragments of the long-lost and about-to-be found Amber Room, the intricate chamber made from amber, a material comprised of honey, linseed, and cognac ..."

"Cognac," I muttered to Arturo, who was busy rolling a cigarette. "He sounds like he's well-infused with cognac."

Unaware of my facetious scoffing, the mayor continued in the typical loud, ranting voice of a politician,

"These panels, about to be unearthed, before they were looted from Russia by the Nazis during the Second World War, were referred to as the eighth wonder of the world."

His passion increased. The veins in his neck bulged and pulsed during his excited ranting. A nervous tittering ran through the crowd.

I stood watching in fascinated horror as his face turned a bright crimson. I gasped as the pulse in his temple accelerated, and his volume crescendoed! He looked as if he were ready to blow. I wondered if I should run for cover as he continued,

"There is reason to believe I have been given the key to unlock one of the most tantalizing mysteries of the war—the Amber Room. I have received documents that provide the precise coordinates of the location. And those coordinates, my friends, point here, to our very own Lake Whalen!"

Saul and Arturo both jabbed me in the ribs and hissed in my ears,

"We need to leave now, while everyone is under the spell of this ranting lunatic. Remember, Arturo and I planted those documents with the coordinates faked to look like Lake Whalen. That way our *Nameless* friends can attach some sort of authenticity to their digging and diving activities."

"Oh, yeah," I said, pulling myself away. The convincing orator had cast his spell over me! As we retreated to the car, we could still hear him. I turned back for a last look and listened,

"Should someone find it, would it be *finders, keepers?* No! The treasure would belong to the state, but the resulting tourism would be a gift. I would love to see the treasure handed back to the Russian people. Maybe in return they would provide the village with just enough reward money to build a new school!"

After he finished shouting, his eyes became glued to the excavation area, where he believed there to be buried several tons of wartime gold, jewels, as well as amber panels. Perhaps his humble hopes would become a reality. Already, tourism was picking up.

While the mayor blathered, the crowds gathered and gawked. We took our leave.

Chapter 59

Treasure hunters refuse to surrender the quest for the Amber Room, reputed to be worth around €350m (£263m) today. They have pumped tens of thousands of euros into the search. When found, it will be interesting to witness who all attempts to claim ownership of the vast treasure.

The Amber Room club, along with other researchers, was seeking permission for an even greater excavation. I had applied for membership to the Amber Room club. I love clubs. After all, I'm a member of the *Philately Fraud Squad.*

It's been several days, but I have not yet heard back concerning my membership application. I'm beginning to get the vibes that the organization is hoity-toity and exclusive.

To qualify for participation, the applicant has to be either German or Russian, be an amber craftsperson, or have intimate knowledge as to where the room is buried. I was of Ukrainian heritage. Maybe that would be close enough.

If I knew where the room was buried, I wouldn't need to join their snooty club. I was beginning to suspect that the organization's members were less than warm and fuzzy.

We had begun this quest with the altruistic desire to return the Lünersee stamps to the owner's heirs. The quest had taken a heavy toll on our finances, and my pathetic resources were particularly hard hit.

Along with all the other fortune hunters, our Spartan life style was beginning to stimulate a craving for wealth— solvency at the very least. We would resist resigning ourselves to the concept of living a debt-filled life.

****

Before leaving for the Lünersee area, we detoured and explored the archives of a church near the area designated by the actual coordinates for the Amber Room. There, we encountered a genteel woman. She happened to be the widow of a history professor, who had also been the local historian.

That is, he was the local historian until his recent and *unexplained* death, which occurred after receiving many death threats. *Odessa*?

It was unlikely to be the *DKDKD*. The *DKDKD's* primary interest was stamps. This treasure was more about the amber room and gold and jewels. Nor did the professor sound like someone who would mishandle stamps. He would, instead, treat them with the reverence they deserved.

The good professor's wife shared with us,

> My Martin always said there was treasure to be found here. We had possessed documents supporting the claim that diamonds, gold and another spectacular treasure lay in a manmade cave near the lake.
>
> But since we used to receive death threats from people wanting to know where the treasure was, we moved the documents to the safe in the town hall, I can now sleep at night without fear. If only Frederick were here to share the peace with me!

It would indeed be sensational if fragments or the actual remains of the Amber Room itself were to be found in this remote area. Amber is now at least *12 times* more valuable than gold. This 60-plus year old treasure quest has fueled endless conspiracy theories, diplomatic rows and expensive searches in everything from lakes to sea beds.

A collaborative effort between the Germans and the Russians to reconstruct the chamber has done little to quell the interest in this extraordinary treasure. Thousands of treasure hunters refuse to believe the Amber Room has been lost forever.

The professor's wife continued. What she said tugged at our heart strings, for it showed what a selfless couple they had been,

> It was the professor's great wish, if the Amber Room were to be found in this little village, based on the information provided by the documents he had safe-guarded for so

long, that the treasure be handed back to the Russian people.
In return, perhaps the Russians would grant to the village just enough reward money to fund the building of a new hospital for the village and to provide a pension for the old villagers who had lived through the travails of the war.

This site, the site pinpointed by the coordinates shared in the documents, was some miles from Lake Whalen and along the German/Austrian border. We vowed to return and conduct a realistic search based on actual data. With that solemn promise, we headed to the Lünersee.

Our quest for the stamps would hopefully reach a successful conclusion.

Chapter 60

Should the Dachau treasure still exist in the Lünersee, the estimated current value, though not as great as the Amber Room, was substantial. The value is something akin to 50,000,000 dollars. Some of the original lake area is once again under water, making the search along the shore line even more difficult.

Yet, there were three of us and we were well-equipped. We maintained a high level of confidence. Each of us would accept responsibility for searching a third of the shore.

All was quiet along the lake front when we arrived later in the day. Our VW was laden with diving gear, tents, food, and a few weapons for protection that we had managed to procure along the way.

I suggested,

"Let's set up camp against one of the rock walls on a ledge above the lake. Maybe there we can escape detection while being able to spot anyone attempting to invade our camp. Evening is approaching, so after setting up camp and stowing our gear, we should begin exploration preparations."

Saul and Arturo agreed. Our strategy was to divide the area to be searched into three sectors. We marked the areas off on the map, expecting to commence with explorations that night. This would be a time when prying eyes would be least likely to track our activities.

Slipping into our wetsuits, goggles and flippers, we carried our air tanks to the area of the search. At last, mouth piece in place, I stepped off into the lake's murky waters, adjusting the headlamp, hoping to scrutinize every square inch of the area.

Technique included prodding deep into the sand and slime every few feet with a rod. At one point, I thought I had struck pay dirt when my probing tool collided with a solid object about a foot deep into the sand, soil, and slime.

My heart skipped a beat, but my cynical nature cautioned against premature celebration. Sure enough, my *treasure*, when exposed, was nothing more than a rock.

After several futile and tedious hours, I resurfaced to find my companions already stripping off their gear, ready to call it a night. It had actually been a day and a night.

Our snack consisted of some cold fruit and cheese. Saul and Arturo had their customary cup of coffee laced with powdered milk. Feeling content with our evening's work, we each crawled into a tent. I collapsed into a deep dreamless sleep.

We spent several days in much the same way, working our way around the perimeter of the lake. It was a race against time.

According to Saul,

> Later this year, they will drain the lake again so that portions of the dam can be repaired. While a lower water level would aid our efforts to scour the perimeter as we seek clues, caves, and ledges where treasure might be stored, it would facilitate other treasure hunters also. We need to keep our activities low profile. People need to think of us as campers, hikers, boaters, so we attract as little attention as possible.

Several days had passed since communicating with our comrades at Lake Whalen. This was one night when sleep did not come easily. Since our searches were proving futile, my curiosity over events on the Whalen front was growing.

I tossed and turned for a while and then popped my head out of my tent, hoping that the others were as sleepless as I. In a loud stage whisper, as though there were others besides us in danger of being awakened, I hissed,

"Hey Saul and Arturo, have you heard anything from the other site?"

My whispered query met with a silence broken only by intermittent snoring.

"Pssst," I hissed, hoping for a response.

Again, I heard nothing other than rasping and labored breathing from the other two tents.

Crawling out from my tent to investigate, I scanned the sky. The high moon enhanced visibility. Erie shadows abounded.

Chapter 61

I first crawled to Arturo's tent and poked my head through the flap. He seemed to be in an unusually deep sleep. I next crawled over to Saul's tent. My efforts revealed a similar situation.

Something was amiss. On a typical night, both were very light sleepers, awakening with the slightest provocation.

I started to enter Saul's tent to take a closer look. It was then that I noticed a figure sitting atop a rock not far from the camp site. His lighted cigarette hissed when he flicked it down into the water. He said,

"Good evening, Fraulein. I was wondering when you would venture out from ze comfort of your tent. Do not worry about your companions. Zey are not dead, but merely in a very deep sleep. Ze drug will wear off in a few hours. You and I will be long gone before zat happens."

Of course, I knew they weren't dead! I could hear their heavy breathing even before I left the comfort of my sleeping bag. Their combined snoring could awaken the dead.

Ignoring the inherent danger of the situation, I crawled closer for a better look. His presence was quite troubling. Something about this stranger's appearance jogged a memory. Besides being an unexpected intruder in our camp, he exuded evilness. Goose bumps appeared on my arms. Not the good kind, either.

Perhaps it was the German accent. Nazis had been on my mind a great deal of late. We were intruding upon their sacred burial grounds—treasure burial grounds I liked to think.

But the shocking truth is that several fortune seekers had vanished during their quests in this locality. Their remains were most likely buried here. Or they had been dumped into the lake.

The stranger's suggestion that I would accompany him to another destination without either of my companions did not sit well with me. I flashed back to Karl and slut-woman's conversation regarding assassination. And I was almost certain that we had met previously.

Screaming was an option, but my companions were still lying stupefied in their tents. Perhaps they had been drugged! And, we were miles from civilization and other living beings.

I would resist. I looked down and then felt a slight wash of relief. When out in the wilderness, I made it a habit of sleeping fully clothed, and I had slipped on my shoes before venturing from the tent.

I am not a gun advocate, far from it. I disavow violence against man or animal, but I am a strong proponent of being prepared to defend myself. For this reason, I always carry a Swiss army knife and a teeny, tiny gun in one of my pockets.

These were procured after disembarking from the ship. I have no idea what the official name or description for my little gun is, but I do know that if I insert it's teeny, tiny clip, and then pull the teeny tiny trigger, it can create a significant hole.

I am squeamish and would have difficulty dealing with the blood and gore associated with a fatal shot. Therefore, I have practiced aiming and nailing knee caps and feet—to debilitate, not to kill. I was fully prepared to do so right now, right this very moment.

I was reaching into my pocket...

The drug's effect must not have been too long-lasting. As if on cue, Arturo and Saul staggered from their tents, aroused by the agitated discourse between the stranger and myself. They were mumbling and staggering about, still somewhat under the effects of whatever drug they had taken.

"Who are you? Why are you here? What are you doing here?" Saul queried, slurring his words together. As he peered at the stranger, recent memories staggered back,

"Wait, weren't you the one who helped us to load our supplies into the VW? You brought the powdered milk out for us, after a long delay, I might add."

My nocturnal visitor looked surprised to see Saul up and about. He then smiled at Saul's struggling memories and inability to articulate in a more coherent manner, but said nothing. Instead, he extracted and lit another cigarette. An eerie silence settled on the group as he sat there, sucking deeply, exhaling... and observing.

Unable to endure the weirdness of the situation any longer, I swallowed my fear and pride. I asked of the stranger,

"What do you want? We don't have much money, but you're welcome to what we have."

I waited for a response, becoming more unraveled by his silence as the minutes slid by. The unsettling stranger took another drag from his cigarette. His look was ponderous.

"Are you hungry?" I asked, trying another approach. That question also went unanswered.

Finally, after inhaling deeply on the cigarette, he asked,

"Fraulein, why are you here?"

"We're here on holiday. And what business is it of yours?"

I lied, although not really. It was a holiday, just a working holiday.

"Why did you pick zis area for your *holiday*," he asked.

"Because of its pristine beauty and because we thought it was isolated here! And it was, until now. Why do you want to know? Is it so unusual for a party to camp on these shores? Are you a land owner here?"

"Nein, zere is a rumor zat a party from the States is heading zis way to search for the Lünersee treasure. I wanted to be here to tell you that zese beaches have been dug up many times, and ze land under ze water close to ze shore has been explored, inch by inch. So if treasure were ever here, it has long since been taken away."

"Is that so?" I murmured.

It seemed most peculiar that, if there were no treasure to be found, he was most anxious for us to depart, in one condition or another. All the while that I had been talking, hoping to distract him, I had been inching the gun from my back pocket. I'm sure it appeared as though I were engaged in some unlady-like scratching.

We sat there in deep suspicion of each other. I scanned the shore lines, with the tiny gun cupped in my hand. On the opposite shore, I could just barely make out a hut through the emerging mist.

It was near the hut that the treasure was alleged to have been buried. How could I have forgotten that?

An idea developed. I reached a decision. We would no longer explore the beaches, but instead would focus on the hut. Perhaps there was a secret panel or floor or basement used to conceal at least part of the treasure.

If I had been hiding loot, I certainly would not stash it all in the same place. I would spread it over several locations. As soon as we rid ourselves of our unwanted guest, we could get started.

Since it had occurred to me that, perhaps, he was the assassin I had heard the Slarls discussing in regard to my fate, I turned to him and asked,

"What did you give Arturo and Saul to make them so dysfunctional? How did you administer it?"

Looking both clever and evil, he whispered in a hoarse monotone,

"I wouldn't be sharing zis wiz you, but none of you is going to be leaving here to tell ze tale, so, as you Americans say, *what ze heck*. I slipped several crushed Xanax tablets into ze powdered milk and yogurt zey purchased. Zose two mentioned dat zey were making pancakes and coffee for dinner tonight. Had you eaten something besides your granola bar, you would be as dopey as zey are."

I looked down at the granola bar wrapper I had dropped outside my tent.

He continued,

"You see, you are all going to have a swimming accident. Such a pity, but not too unusual a fate for treasure hunters exploring ze lakes in zese regions. No one will be ze least bit suspicious, eh?"

I was convinced now that he was the assassin that I had overheard the Slarls discussing on the boat. For a time, I had suspected Neal, the Navigation Officer, since he had almost knocked me over the boat's railing.

Becoming more than annoyed by the sleazy grin on this weirdo's face, with one swift motion, I brought up my teeny, tiny gun and took aim. Caught by surprise, he had no time to react.

Grimacing, I shot the bloody Nazi supporter (assumption) in the left knee-cap. Next, I shot him in his right foot. As he rolled on the ground in pain, I attempted to sober up Art and Saul by dousing them with frigid lake water. Not a perfect solution, but at least they were no longer staggering about, slurring their words.

Grabbing the rope we used to suspend our food supply from trees when, on occasion, we hiked in to a campsite, I grabbed and bound the suspected *Odessa* member's arms behind him.

Pounding a spare tent stake into the rocky ground, I attached the rope used to fasten his hands to the stake and then pounded the rod further into the ground. It was a smooth dowel. There were no rough surfaces or angular edges for him to use to fray the rope and escape.

This was precautionary. He was in such agony from his incapacitated knee and foot that I suspected escape was secondary to his need for pain-relieving medication.

While attaching him to the tent stake, I happened to look down at his feet and his shoes. Wait! I knew those shoes. Now the memory came flooding back.

He was the one who had captivated his philatelic cruise audience with the fascinating Middle Eastern stamp lecture.

He was the one who had covered the stamp I was trying to retrieve on the ship's deck with his highly polished shoe and then walked off. How could I ever forget those pointy-tip shoes?

The current occasion called for some very strong black coffee for Arturo and Saul and me. I also brewed a cup for our visitor. His was diluted with the Xanax-adulterated dried milk.

We sat there waiting for our black coffee and the coffee with mucho Xanax-milk to have their opposing effects. The prisoner began to relax and soon ceased writhing and moaning from his gun-inflicted injuries.

Saul and Arturo gradually regained their faculties. When my two companions were able to say Lünersee stamps five times in rapid succession, I judged them to be sober enough.

Our uninvited guest's head soon slumped onto his chest, drool dripping from his mouth. His snoring soon rivaled the sounds of an approaching freight train.

My coffee was a success, a surprising accomplishment for me.

Saul, now alert enough to shift his mind into an analytical mode, recommended that we pack all camping supplies, including tents. We would load them into the canoe we had brought for exploring different areas of the lake. Then we would paddle to the opposing shore where the hut was.

"What about him?" Arturo gestured with his head at the slumbering uninvited guest.

"Hmm. What about him?" I shrugged.

Arturo, always a softy, said,

"We can't just leave him there. He'll starve, or some animal will attack him."

"Yes?" I shrugged.

Saul smiled. Arturo stared, aghast.

"Relax," I said. "After we search the hut, we'll return to the village and tell them where to find Heinrich or whatever his name is. He'll be okay here for a few hours while he sleeps off the *Xanax* he added to the milk to drug us. We only survived because I just don't happen to drink coffee before I turn in for the night."

Arturo looked somewhat reassured and commenced helping Saul load our gear into the canoe. I would sit in the center and keep watch while Arturo and Saul paddled.

I sat facing the sleeping prisoner while Saul and Arturo struggled to coordinate their paddling. Despite their clumsy efforts, the distance between us and the shore with its unconscious captive was increasing.

By the time we reached the opposing shore, clouds began to obscure the moon, our sole light source. The mist, stirred by an increasing breeze, grew denser.

We emptied our packs of unnecessary gear, taking only our flashlights and a few tools. Our method for determining who would be the first to stand guard was less than scientific. We played Rock, Paper, Scissors.

The two *losers* would enter the shack, examining it for secret tunnels and hiding places. Our theory was that since no one had found treasure in or along the lake, we would pursue the concept that the treasure, or at least a part of it, was buried in a secret chamber under the hut.

Arturo drew the first watch and so assumed a position where he could observe the canoe as well as the shoreline. He stood with his back against a sheer rock face.

One of us, if we hadn't discovered anything in twenty minutes, would relieve him. We would continue rotating in such a manner until we either found something or decided to abandon the project.

Chapter 62

Saul and I, assuming that Heinrich was not acting alone, theorized that we had little time to linger. We scrambled up the path leading to the hut without further ado. The trail presented a steep climb, leaving us breathless by the time we reached our destination.

The old structure, perched on a rock shelf, was larger than we had thought. Its back wall, obscured from view from below, extended deep into a recess in the rock face. Its single window was shuttered. They were nailed down tight.

The heavy wood plank door was padlocked. Further perusal exposed a chimney that might suffice as a port of entry should we be unable to free the door or window. We would use that recourse only if we wished to run the risk of meeting an exiting raccoon.

A close examination of the structure indicated that it had been unused for many years. Arturo had responded to the signal we sent him to ensure that he was taking his watch role seriously.

We emptied our sparse collection of tools onto the ground and commenced with the break in. I began prying the nails from the shutters while Saul attempted to pick the padlock on the door.

Our goal was to gain access and conduct a thorough search of the structure before dawn. We moved about our tasks with haste, continuing to be as quiet as possible.

I, at last, had loosened one of the shutters, beckoning Saul over to assist. Just then, a few stones rattled down the rock face. Startled, we froze.

After a moment, we summoned the courage to look up. In our agitation, we expected to see either a bear or a lynx ready to pounce, or a Nazi believer pointing a rifle our way.

What a relief to see a petite mountain goat mama and her little kid picking their way across the precarious heights. They were, no doubt, traipsing to a special alpine pasture, a certain indication that dawn would soon be approaching.

We picked up our pace. Saul helped me wrench a shutter open: first one and then the other. We peered through the opening. Any glass was long gone.

Saul pulled out his flashlight. There were the expected crude chairs and table in the center of the area. The room was devoid of cobwebs, perhaps due to the harsh climate, but maybe an indication that others had been here before us? We could see little else in the gloom.

After gathering our equipment and dropping it onto the floor of the room, we hoisted ourselves up and over the sill. Saul had the foresight to position the shutters back over the window.

From a distance the cabin still appeared to be abandoned. With the shutters closed, we both turned on our lights and began looking for a trap door in the floor.

The floor was seamless; no hidden entry was apparent. As we examined the walls, an idea began to form,

"Do you think it's somewhat unusual for the back of the cabin to extend so far into the recess of the rock face?" I asked Saul.

"Yeah, I noticed that too," he said as he moved closer to the shelving on the far wall.

Reaching the same conclusion, we both began to pull and press on the boards of the book shelf lining the back wall. Nothing happened.

We tried lifting, thinking that if we removed them, we could examine the wall itself. When that plan failed, I began taking away the heavy, dust-laden crockery and jars, placing them on the floor and the table.

I was boosting one extremely heavy piece, when I heard a sudden, harsh grinding noise. I almost dropped the heavy crock in fright.

Disconcerted, we turned off our flashes and stood perfectly still. The unusual grating continued for several seconds more. Then, once again, there was just eerie silence.

Several moments passed. After hearing nothing additional, we switched the flashlights back on. There was a wafting of cool air on my ankles. I directed the light down to find the source.

The bottom shelves had slid back just enough to reveal a small crawl space. The entry operated on principles that were the reverse of what we had been expecting.

As long as a heavy object like the large crock I had just lifted depressed the lever embedded in the shelving, the concealed entry remained closed. Removing the heavy piece of pottery released the lever and exposed the entrance.

Overcome with curiosity, Saul stooped down and shone his light inside. Unable to see beyond a couple of feet, he first stuck in his arm to develop an impression of the environment. Then, amidst muffled huffing and groaning, he clambered in.

Beset with curiosity and excitement, I ignored my claustrophobia and soon followed. The narrow passageway was rough and winding, continuing for quite some distance. It sloped upwards the entire way.

Just when we had begun to think that we had discovered nothing more than a tunnel, a huge, cavernous room opened before us. The chamber was typical of many caves, except for the unusual number of passages leading off the main room, all in different directions.

The sheer number was sufficient to ensure a time-consuming and difficult search. We decided to explore each one, regretting that Arturo was not here to help. I would start from the right, Saul from the left.

"Maybe we should go together?" I asked with a sudden feeling of trepidation.

"Did I mention that I'm claustrophobic?"

Saul said,

"Schnell!"

So we each selected a passage. I was hoping not to encounter a situation like Davy Jones' Locker, a chamber littered with decades old skeletons.

As I plodded along, I heard a faint *Yeehaa!* Thinking it was Saul, I retraced my steps, stumbling and tripping a time or two in my haste.

When I reached the large room, I shouted,

"What did you find?"

My voice reverberated.

I then heard another whoop from the passage on the far left, the one Saul had taken. I scuttled along. That tunnel soon opened into another room where I came to an abrupt halt.

There, far in front of me, I could see two individuals. After a moment, each turned. Their faces were visible in the light from the lanterns perched on rocks a short distance away.

There in the dim, flickering light was none other than Neal, the navigation officer from the cruise ship. Beside him was slut-woman, Mindy, the über Ukrainian. In the dancing light of the cavern, her huge breasts appeared to be heaving.

Slut-woman was decked out in the sparkling baubles she had pulled from a nearby box that had a huge swastika emblazoned on its side. Neal was filling a backpack with gold coins and more jewelry.

In all their merriment, neither had noticed Saul nor me as we crouched behind a stalagmite. In fact, I hadn't noticed Saul until he tugged on my pant leg, motioning for me to hunker down beside him.

It must have been they who were creating all the noise and sounds of revelry that drew me back from my exploratory duties. Thank goodness my response whoop had gone unnoticed.

There must be another entrance to this cavern. That, of course, would not be unusual. Caves often have multiple accesses.

Were slut-woman and Neal Heinrich allies? What was slut-woman doing with Neal? Where was Karl? Had Mindy needed him only until the treasure was found, as I had feared? And to think that I had shown Neal my, uh, coordinates!

Neal and slut-woman seemed unconcerned about being overheard or discovered. Perhaps they assumed that Heinrich had disposed of us according to plan. There was enough loot in this one cavern to keep them occupied for some time as they made multiple trips back and forth.

"What do you suggest?" I queried of Saul.

Conferring in whispers, we agreed that a confrontation would be counterproductive. They were, no doubt, armed themselves. They also might have allies close by.

I weighed the options and then thought,

Perhaps we can create a distraction causing them to abandon this site. Then we can continue with our own explorations.

Leaving Saul to keep an eye on the situation, I retraced my steps to the cabin. With a minimal amount of reception, I managed to text our allies at Lake Whalen explaining the situation and our needs.

With renewed hope, I reentered the crawl space from the hut, making certain this time to close the opening behind me.

In the several moments it took me to send the message, Saul had returned to the large outer room in the cavern. As I approached, I noticed his determined expression,

"Whatever it is you did worked. Mindy and Neal came back for one final load. As they were leaving, they were chattering about heading over to Lake Whalen. It seems they overheard on an open channel our *Nameless* Friends exchanging information with other treasure hunters about the possibility of having discovered the Amber Room."

"Great," I said, "That trip should occupy them long enough for us to inspect the other passages."

"But," interjected Saul,

"Before they left, I also heard them laughing. They were chattering about how surprised Arturo would be when he learned that it was they who would soon own his magazine. *He would soon be working for them.*"

"Yikes! You've got to be kidding! I could *never* work for a person like her."

How humiliating it would be to have Neal as my boss after the evening we spent together. I kept that thought to myself.

Chapter 63

It was a discouraging search. We had yet to discover additional treasure, even after exploring all other passages. Perhaps Mindy and Neal had discovered the only wealth hidden at this site.

I rolled my eyes in frustration, feeling outmaneuvered once again by Mindy Slutkowski, and now Neal.

"For Karl's sake, I hope that his friends have *not* discovered the stamps or the Amber Room. I'm afraid that once slut-woman has knowledge of their whereabouts, Karl will be history, if he isn't already. She'll arrange a diving accident or some other type of unfortunate occurrence for him."

For once, rolling my eyes had a positive result. Recessed above a precarious ledge, several feet above the floor of the large chamber, there appeared another opening.

The only access to this aperture was from an overhead ledge. One of us needed to scramble up with the climbing rope, anchor it and then drop one end down for the other to climb.

I stared at Saul until he *volunteered* to lead. While he was in the process of free climbing, I decided that rather than concealing our gear in the large room, it would be prudent to take it with us.

When Saul finally reached the destined area and dropped down one end of the rope we had brought, I tied each of our packs onto it. I signaled for him to haul them up.

When the packs were safely secured on the ledge, he again dropped down the rope end. I pulled myself up and over the ledge to where Saul stood.

And not a moment too soon! We heard footsteps and voices echoing from the chamber where we had left Mindy and Neal. Saul quickly pulled up the rope and removed the tied end from the stalagmite.

The intruders were, of course, Neal and Mindy. They must have decided to scrounge around for treasure one final time before leaving for Lake Whalen.

As their light scanned the walls, we ducked into the small opening. We could only hope they wouldn't see us or decide to explore any further.

After a few moments, when the sound of their voices receded, Saul and I ventured deeper into the passageway. Our expectations were low. So far, the only treasures seemed to be in Mindy and Neal's possession.

We saved our batteries by using the lights only when necessary, groping our way along in the dark. Darkness and silence were soon our sole companions.

After a while, we detected a difference in the air quality, and, when we reached to feel the walls of the passage, we had difficulty. Saul switched on his flashlight to determine what lay ahead. We needed to assess the area for hazards.

We turned a bend, and what we saw left us speechless. I switched on my light as we both stared in awe. It was a vision even more spectacular than description. It was man-made perfection, a spectacle rivaled only by nature.

There before us, in all its glory, appeared the reassembled Amber Room. The cave environment must have served to preserve it. Why it had been reconstructed rather than left in shipping crates was something of a mystery. Perhaps survivors of the horrible Nazi reign of terror drew comfort and encouragement from the ambience created with this magnificent work of art.

After a time, we recovered from the *shock and awe*. We regained our bearings after witnessing the reassembled masterpiece, one long supposed to have been destroyed.

It was then that I spotted an amber table in the middle of the modest-sized chamber. Perhaps it was one of the original furnishings.

On that exquisite table rested an envelope. Saul and I stared at each other for a moment. Taking the lead, I crept to the table, walking as if surrounded by shards of glass, and careful to disturb nothing.

After several apprehensive moments, I reached the table unscathed. Saul bathed the area in the light from his lantern. I lifted the envelope from the table, staring at it for just a moment before scurrying back to where Saul waited.

I survived the trip. Neither chasms opened nor spikes emerged from the walls and ceiling. Whew!

We both looked at the envelope, and then at each other. The envelope bore the words *Addressee Unknown: Return to Sender.*

The hand writing appeared to be identical to the last message. I was referring to the message that had arrived in my mailbox before I had embarked on this latest adventure.

That was the message that contained the picture with the coordinates. That envelope also bore the message: *Addressee Unknown.* Perhaps the puzzle pieces were coming together.

Guilt overrode speculation and excitement. It seemed unfair that Saul and I were experiencing this adventure while Arturo was left at the lake's edge, contemplating our fortune or fate.

Nor was it prudent to have left Arturo alone for this length of time with the Slarls, and now Neal, on the prowl. It was also possible that Heinrich's comrades may have liberated him.

Saul and I took a few photos of the room to prove that we had indeed discovered the masterpiece. I tucked the unopened mystery envelope into my pocket, fully expecting to read its contents once the three of us were situated somewhere safe.

We went but a short distance when skepticism overtook us. We became indecisive. The design of the Amber Panels was to represent the five senses. Sight and touch, I could rationalize, but how did taste, sound and smell come into play?

"Now, Saul, I ask you, should we go over and test the panels... I mean, actually touch them to better understand the representation of the five senses?"

Saul rubbed his once again grizzled chin before offering his considered response,

"We should walk over, but with the greatest of caution. We have no idea if the area closer to the panels is booby trapped. My guess would be that it is."

And so we did—walk over. We tread with caution, ever watchful for a sudden drop off or a loose stone that would trigger some dire effect.

Saul chose to follow me, *to cover our backs*, as he explained. All the while, I pondered, studying the magnificent creation, trying to determine how the panels represented all five senses.

After several moments of continuous walking, we seemed to be no closer to our brilliant goal. Feeling a sense of exasperation, fueled by exhaustion, fear, and hunger, I stopped and stomped my foot in frustration.

The previous dense silence morphed into the sound of an ever increasing thunder of cascading rocks. We could hear them sliding down, down, down, but never heard anything hit bottom.

Remaining perfectly still, afraid even to breathe, with the aid of the lantern we saw to our horror the ever widening crevice created by my tantrum. It took additional time, a seeming eternity, to side step the widening opening.

We proceeded at snail's pace, while accessing the safety of each step before continuing. I reached out to see if, at last, I could touch the glowing surfaces.

My hands swished through empty air. Deflated with disappointment, I queried,

"Well, what do we do now?"

Saul, sounding as exasperated as I, suggested that we should look for clues, either in the hologram or somewhere in the vicinity of the hologram. The only clue seemed to be the one I already had in my hands.

Looking further, we shone our lights, this time not at the walls, but at the floor. In horror we stared in silence at a sheer drop off. Creeping closer, shining our light straight down, we could see no bottom.

If we had continued for just a few additional feet, we would have accompanied the plunging rocks from the slide I had triggered.

It was then that we realized that we were intended victims. We had been captivated by a deception, a hologram, an ingenious facade. The room beyond the table with the envelope had been but an illusion. An illusion designed to lure us to sudden death.

The panels were but a sham created with complex technology. Technical *Odessa* members must be behind this charade, utilizing modern expertise in a most ingenious way.

With our knees shaking, a phenomenon known to climbers as *sewing machine* legs, we retraced our steps, exercising even greater caution. A seeming eternity passed.

Our anxiety still at a high level, we once again stood on the ledge above the large cavernous room. There, we paused in the darkness, assessing for other dangers. It was as quiet as a tomb. Saul flashed his light for the briefest of moments to determine how best to descend.

We both donned our packs. Saul held the rope while I, feeling grateful to be alive, descended. Saul untied and dropped down the rope. I re-coiled it as he descended by touch rather than sight, feeling for the handholds and footholds in the dark.

Once again on solid ground, we scurried along the passage leading to the hut. We were long overdue and apprehensive for Arturo's safety. I began speculating and murmured that I should have left my weapons with him.

Saul chortled,

"It is good that you didn't... he would have shot himself in the foot or put a hole in the boat, for sure."

That single moment of levity sent us into gales of hysterical laughter. Our brush with death had found an emotional outlet.

Chapter 64

Descending from the cavern opening, down the rock face to the lake shore, took several long moments. Some consider descent as being easier than an ascent.

In fact, it is much more precarious. Handholds and footholds are difficult to utilize while descending, which is the reason for using the rappelling technique. Rappelling, or abseiling, is the controlled descent down a rock face using a rope and a harness. Climbers employ this method when a cliff or slope is too steep or dangerous to descend without protection.

Arriving at the bottom with just a few minor scratches and scrapes, we hustled over to the lake shore where we had left Arturo. Since we were gone much longer than anticipated, we could only hope that he was still okay.

Arturo was a reticent individual and not one to take many physical risks if they could be avoided. It wasn't because he was a coward or incapable. He just preferred exertions of the intellectual nature.

On occasion, he would make vague references to his difficult childhood in Poland. Perhaps, those experiences were responsible for his unwillingness to share personal details.

We walked many yards in each direction. I shouted out to Saul, who was in the lead,

"Do you see him?"

Saul shook his head and shrugged. Arturo was nowhere to be seen and the canoe was missing.

I theorized,

"Maybe he became bored and decided to paddle around and explore the lake."

That explanation sounded hollow to both of us. Before sounding an alarm to our comrades at Lake Whalen the decoy treasure hunters, we decided to search for Arturo a little longer. In the meantime, Saul encouraged me to open the envelope. Hesitant, perhaps fearful of what was in the envelope, perhaps the time and date of Armageddon, I began to argue,

"How do I know it's meant for me? It says *Addressee Unknown: Return to Sender*. It just so happens that the *Sender* is unknown too."

"We'll never know unless you open it, and, besides, the clues arriving in your mailbox were addressed in a similar fashion. You opened that. Maybe you are the *Addressee Unknown*."

I pried the flap loose. After a moment and with a little cry, I sank to my knees.

When my eyes snapped open, I was surrounded. There were Saul and several of my *Nameless* companions hovering, all with concerned and solicitous expressions. I must have been out for quite some time. Before I could say a word, Saul took the lead,

"Elyse, how do you feel? You passed out after you looked at the *Addressee Unknown* envelope contents. And you have had such a tight grasp on the letter that we haven't been able to pry it from your fingers. Let's all take a look so that we can understand what's so upsetting to you."

Surveying my clenched hands, I could see that Saul wasn't exaggerating. The whitened knuckles of both hands were beginning to ache from my vice-like grasp on the folded paper. Still speechless, I struggled to a sitting position. Releasing my grip, I unfolded the paper. Inside was a picture. I gave another gasp.

It was a picture of Karl sitting, bound and gagged with duct tape in what appeared to be a cave. Were those etchings on the cave walls behind him?

Propped against him was an open album. The album did not contain photographs. The pages were filled with neatly arranged stamps. They had every appearance of being antiquated stamps. Their edges were yellowed with age and would have curled had they not been mounted in such a meticulous manner.

Upon closer scrutiny, I recognized a few. They were among the rarest and most valuable stamps in the world.

Once again, I scrutinized the picture. At first glance I had assumed that the bound and gagged figure was Karl. But the photo quality was not good. The somewhat blurred figure also bore a faint resemblance to Arturo, minus his glasses, who was also missing.

If only we knew where he was!

I groaned. Saul, the person in closest proximity, snatched the paper and photo from my hands. He then showed it to the others. Sympathetic murmuring began:

"Don't worry, Edna... or Elyse, we'll find him."

"It's possible that he's still alive, Ethel," someone else shouted.

"Shocking, who could have done this," murmured another.

"It's a poor quality picture. Do you think slut-woman took it?"

"He may still be alive. We can only hope."

I shouted,

"No! Don't you see the stamps in the picture? These must be the fabled Lünersee stamps. Do you see the faded date and location imprints in German on the bottom of the pages? This is the first clear indication we have that the stamps aren't just a legend."

I went on to explain,

"The picture reveals at least two pages of the collection. Now, at least, we have the identity of some of them! In fact, we have enough information to be able to identify the entire collection, unless of course, they've split them up.

"The collection would lose considerable value under those circumstances. It's the legend and the decades old search that contribute to their value."

I slumped to the ground, once again overcome with the overwhelming realization that, at last, we could identify the legendary collection. But to find them, we had to find Karl, assuming that he was still alive.

Perhaps now, with the dawning realization that he had been but a pawn in slut-woman's schemes, he would point an incriminating finger at her.

Arturo would lose a buyer for his magazine, but wasn't that for the best—for him and me? At the moment that detail seemed insignificant.

My mind rambled on. Of course, if the stamps in the picture were the entire collection, we could devote our attention to the fabled Amber Room.

I love that room!

Before engaging in any of those pursuits, we must first find Arturo. Only then, can we focus on Karl and the stamps in earnest. To find Karl, or, perhaps, Arturo, we have only the photograph to guide us.

I called over to Saul, who had been smoking and chatting with the *Nameless* group. Showing him the picture once again, I said, "Are those the petroglyphs found in the Lascaux Caves in France on the cavern walls behind him?"

Author Biography — Janet Feduska Cole

Growing up with little television, but ready access to fields, streams, and woods, had turned me into a young, female Tom Sawyer of sorts. My childhood companions, Marsha, Mikey, and I spent the summers exploring, playing in fields, woods, and streams, doing our best to stay out of the clutches of our mothers with their long lists of chores, which included seeding, then weeding huge gardens, hanging clothes out to dry on washday (Mondays always), ironing our father's starched white work shirts, or pulling weeds out of the huge lawns.

When we grew old enough to attend school and become boring student drones, I, who had developed a love for music, was given a flute for some birthday or other. Through intense practicing, with a smidgeon of talent, I became quite proficient. This love for music, because it allowed me to be individualistic—creating a signature tone and style, accounts for my spending one semester as a conservatory music student in an urban Pittsburgh University.

But, I was a country girl, and missed the wide open spaces, and trees, and streams. Nor did I have a vision for myself as a musician. So, I transferred to Penn State in countrified Happy Valley, where my brother and sister also happened to be students. There, I studied Microbiology, a field in which I worked for more than eight years. During this period, my love for the outdoors and addiction to adventure led me to participate in scuba diving, rock and mountain climbing, and hiking adventures.

After taking a few years off to start an all-boy family (two sons and a husband), I re-evaluated and returned to school to earn an MBA. My resistance to working full-time during my children's tender years lead me into project work, which included technical writing—a field that I currently pursue full-time. It is only in recent years that I have begun to harness my imagination and quest for adventure, channeling these traits into creative skit productions, a short story, and now my second published novel.

Coming Soon

The Whistleblower's Concierge

The third novel in the Nazi Treasure mystery series, Elyse assumes a new responsibility, that of protecting the most recent of the whistleblowers. In their flight from government teams of assassins, Elyse and Peter, the whistleblower, become acquainted with the mysterious Allagash Wilderness. After ensuring Peter's safe passage to a sympathetic country, Elyse, Saul and Arturo continue their treasure quests. Fresh obstacles include a new, but no less avaricious generation of the Knights Templars.

www.ingramcontent.com/pod-product-compliance
Lightning Source LLC
Chambersburg PA
CBHW031421250626
47155CB00004B/1571